ALONG THE OLD PIER

JACK BENTON

AMMFA
PUBLISHING

ALSO BY JACK BENTON

The Slim Hardy Mystery Series

The Man by the Sea

The Clockmaker's Secret

The Games Keeper

Slow Train

The Angler's Tale

Eight Days

When the Wind Blows

The Circus Lights

Here the Road Ends

Along the Old Pier

The Tokyo Lost Series

Broken

Frozen

Stolen

For Vicky Bagley

AUTHOR'S NOTE

I have taken some considerable liberties with the locations described in this book, as well as amending their respective histories to suit my fictional needs.

Forgive me…

ALONG THE OLD PIER

THE WIND SEEMED insistent on ripping the coat from John "Slim" Hardy's shoulders. As he followed limping Reggie Bowles along the promenade towards the pier sticking out into the grey, choppy water of the Bristol Channel, he struggled to see quite what people found attractive about these seaside towns. He'd stepped on a discarded fish 'n' chips wrapper, almost stepped on a dead seagull, and had an ownerless terrier of some kind attempt to urinate on his leg. Although it was early May, with summer on the grey, indistinct horizon, few local businesses appeared to be preparing for the coming summer season. Many were boarded up, or had only jagged shards of glass remaining in their windows, their signs faded or taken down, which suggested that they might not open up at all.

'I found him just down there, on the sand,' Reggie said, leaning over the low promenade wall to point at the shadowy triangle beneath the struts of the pier extending out from the promenade a stone's throw up ahead. 'He used to nap down there sometimes on warm days, out of the sun, hand behind his head like, so at first I thought he was sleeping. Didn't occur to me that the old guy might be dead.'

Reggie continued along the promenade, and then descended a set of concrete, sand-buried steps down onto the beach. Aside from a few hardy dog walkers, hands stuffed deep into their pockets, coats zipped up to their necks, the flat sand surrounding the pier, stretching out into the sea, was empty. A few glass bottles, washed up by the grey waves, protruded out of the wet sand. A crushed food container tumbled over and over, propelled by the biting wind that would gust then pause, gust then pause, in an endless cycle like it was having difficulty breathing.

Slim stood for a moment at the top of the steps, looking down at the beach. The Grand Pier stretched three hundred yards out into the sea, a wooden platform protected by a rusting metal railing, to where a gaudy bulb of entertainment sat like a spaceship that had just landed, propped up by dozens of water-stained wooden stilts that from this distance looked too spindly to support its weight. In water at high tide and mud at low, now with the sea halfway out, gentle waves lapped and sloshed around them, sending up plumes of white spray.

The narrow triangle of space below where the pier's walkway connected with the promenade gradually widened as the beach stretched away. Closest to the concrete promenade, the triangular hollow appeared to be in perpetual shadow, the sand damp and green with algae and patches of sun-shy couch grass. Reggie had stopped at the bottom of the steps and was pointing into that dank, murky area. Slim found it hard to believe how anyone could have taken comfort squeezed up into that place. Besides having a little shelter from the wind and rain, it more closely resembled a tomb. That a man had died in this space didn't surprise Slim at all. The surprise lay in what Reggie told him next.

Slim continued down the steps until he was standing beside Reggie. 'Tell me again about Bob,' Slim said.

'He was the last of a kind,' Reggie said, his voice tinged with a note of sadness. 'He'd done the Punch and Judy along this beach for fifty years.' He gave a little chuckle. 'Until I found him dead, I would have thought it more likely the beach would weather around him,' Reggie said.

Slim recalled how he had met Reggie. After a signing event at a local bookshop in late April, where he had been reluctantly promoting a ghostwritten book on one of his cases, a man had nearly bundled into him as he exited the shop. Clearly recognising him, Reggie had grabbed his shoulders and practically shouted into his face. 'Mr Hardy, please, I need to speak to you,' he had said, and the look in his eyes had made it impossible for Slim to refuse.

Always preferring the quiet confines of a backstreet café to anywhere bustling with people, Slim invited the man for coffee. About to close, the café had just enough left in the filter to satisfy Slim's craving. With a strong black coffee in front of him, he had listened to Reggie's story.

'We were friends going back decades,' Reggie said. 'I might look old to you, but to Bob I was always just "the boy". Even though I'd been sweeping and picking litter up along that promenade for nearly thirty years, Bob still looked on me like a youngster to take under his wing. And even though it might have looked on the outside like the old guy never smiled, it weren't true. Many a night we'd go down there at sunset after the crowds were gone and drink a beer and talk about the day. He was a good sort, Bob was.'

'Did he live locally?' Slim asked, sipping at his coffee. 'I suppose he must've done, to have worked here for so long.'

'I believe he had a place, somewhere across town,' Reggie said. 'But he was down around the pier so much of his time, that you wondered if he ever went home.'

'Can you tell me about when you found him?' Slim asked.

'I hadn't seen him all day,' Reggie said. 'I wasn't so much worried, but he wasn't the type to go off sick. Served in the Falklands, so he told me, though I can't say if that was true or not. He might have been spinning me a yarn.' Reggie sighed. 'Anyways, I come looking, and I see him up there as always, curled up like he's asleep. Only when I lean in to look, I see a big dark stain on his clothes, and I realise his eyes are wide open and staring at me. He was dead. I felt his wrist, and he's cold, like he's been there for hours.'

'What did you do? Did you call for help?'

'Like, it was about six o'clock and there weren't many people about. Wind was getting up, which always keeps people at home. I went up the road to the phone box, called the police.'

'How long were you gone?'

'Oh, must have been thirty minutes. It's a walk up there now they don't have many around, plus I didn't have no change. Had to ask in a couple of pubs before I got some.' He shrugged. 'Then it took a couple of goes to make the call. Me hands were shaking, see.'

'And then you went back to wait?'

'Yeah. I was gone about half an hour.'

'And when you got back?'

Reggie sighed again. 'See, that's the real mystery isn't it? When I got back, he was gone.'

2

'I'LL JUST HAVE a small bag of chips,' Slim said to the man at the service window of the little shop at the entrance to the pier. Three p.m. and he wasn't hungry, a sandwich and a coffee propping him up from earlier. The wind, though, was biting and cold, defying all but a handful of hardy tourists wandering up and down the pier.

'You local?' Slim asked the man as he scooped chips into a cardboard container. 'And could you wrap those in newspaper if you have it?' He smiled. 'I have a penchant for the old days, the way they used to taste.'

The man nodded. A bushy moustache lifted as he returned Slim's smile.

'Those are words I hear less and less,' he said. 'I'll do you greaseproof on the outside in case the inspector comes past, yesterday's news on the inside. I've got old coffee if you need some. It would be wrong to charge you for it.'

'I'd pay extra for old,' Slim said. 'Ideally yesterday's.'

'Give me a sec. Right. Here you go. And to answer your question, kind of. Born here, moved away young, moved back old. This was my dad's place. Mum ran off with a train conductor, then when in his turn, he ran off, she caught the train back, begged for a second chance. The old man was a mug; she gambled away two of his shops before she died, leaving just this one. I took it over when he got too old, but I'm getting that way myself now.'

'This is going to sound like a line, but I work for the BBC. My name's Mike Lewis.'

The moustache tilted at one side. 'Richard Hardberry. What can I help you with, Mr Lewis?'

'I'm researching for a documentary on seaside performers. Traditional types. I hear there's a Punch and Judy man around here. I know it's early in the year, but I thought he might be wandering about somewhere.'

'Ah, you must mean Bob Harker. He's the only one I know of. Not seen him in a while but I heard he's gone missing.'

Slim tried to look surprised. 'Is that right?'

'Supposedly. Can't say I know much about it. I saw a police car, though. Heard a commotion. The gossip usually reaches me eventually but I heard it was old Reggie Bowles who called it in, and without meaning to be rude,' Richard leaned forward, glancing up and down the pier, then lowered his voice, 'he's a sandwich short of a picnic, if you know what I mean.'

'This Reggie … he's also local?' Slim asked, deciding to play dumb for now.

'I suppose so.' Richard frowned, staring off into the distance as he wiped his hands on a dishcloth. 'He's defi-nitely a local boy.'

Slim remembered how Reggie had described Bob's way of referring to him.

'Does he live around here?' he asked, casting out his line to see what he could catch.

Richard leaned out of the booth window and pointed up the street.

'Yeah, he sure does. I could write down his address but there wouldn't be much point. He lives up there, number 124. The first floor window is his room, so I believe.'

'The first floor...?' Slim muttered, having wondered how someone as scruffy as Reggie Bowles could afford to live in one of the seafront properties he had seen advertised in local estate agents for sums in excess of half a million pounds.

'Yes. I suppose you'd call it a residential care home.'

'Reggie ... he works near here?'

Richard chuckled. 'Oh no, not at all. He just thinks he does.'

3

DESPITE BEING PUT off by the unreliability of his only witness, Slim decided to brave the insufferable weather for a few more days, just to see if the lead went anywhere. Staying in a shabby, budget guesthouse a few streets from the beach, he had an ideal base while he pursued the truth in what Reggie Bowles had claimed.

The wind was unrelenting as he walked the length of grey sand, close enough to the shoreline that it was dense and firm beneath his feet. The air smelled of salt and the cries of gulls were never far away. A dog barked. Someone nearby lifted his arm and a piece of driftwood spun through the air. The dog barked again, then raced in pursuit, paws pattering across wet sand, leaving a trail of footprints in its wake. Slim stood and watched for a moment, hands in his pockets, rubbing cold fingers against each other, then headed back to the promenade in search of hot coffee.

Once ensconced in a café window seat out of the wind and the cold, a black coffee on the Formica tabletop in front of him, he called Donald Lane, an old friend from his

Armed Forces days. Don, who had often helped Slim in the past, now ran an intelligence agency in London.

'Slim? That you?'

'It's me, Don. How are you doing?'

'Oh, the same, you know.' Don gave a dry chuckle. 'I read your book. I appreciate not being mentioned.'

It was Slim's turn to chuckle. 'I had very little to do with it.'

'Still shunning the limelight, then? With your track record, I don't know why you don't retire from detective work and do after-dinner speaking. I imagine the food's a lot better than what you live on most of the time.'

'You flatter me,' Slim said. 'I'd probably miss the work too much.'

'What can I do for you today?'

'I'm looking for the address of a man called Bob Harker. Maybe Robert? I tried the phone book but he wasn't listed.'

'No problem. Give me a rough area to work with and I'll see what I can find.'

'Sure.'

Slim gave Don what few details he could and then hung up.

After finishing his coffee, he wandered along the promenade until he came to a small tourist information kiosk. Little more than a booth, a young, bespectacled woman gave him a smile as he leaned into the kiosk window.

'Sorry to bother you,' he said, then gave a sheepish smile. 'I'm a bit of a traditionalist. I was wondering if there's anything like a Punch and Judy show on around here? Old school entertainment, if you like.'

The woman frowned and shook her head. 'Not that I know of,' she said. 'There's an Odeon on Newton Street if you want something that kids might enjoy.'

'No pop-up kind of theatre, anything like that?'

'Well, there was a man who used to wander about on the beach near the pier. You could have a look, see if he's still there. It might be a little early in the season for it, though.'

'Okay, thanks.'

She smiled again. 'If you're looking for something traditional, you could try the amusement arcade on the pier. It has those old-style one-armed bandits, things like that.'

'Thanks, I might.'

Slim headed off. He was beginning to get the impression that Bob Harker was some kind of freelancer, an old-fashioned travelling minstrel type rather than a paid council employee. Perhaps he had fallen foul of the wrong kind of people, maybe hawked his puppetry wares on someone else's turf. Slim remembered reading an article on so-called ice cream van wars. He had considered it laughable until he met a man who'd been beaten up for plying his trade in the wrong part of town. Could such rivalry exist in the Punch and Judy world?

Before getting too deeply into Bob Harker's background, Slim decided to dig into the truth about Reggie's claim a little more. He located a local library, logged onto a computer and did a search of local news reports. To his surprise, he found nothing listed on the websites of any of the local newspapers. However, the library held paper copies dating back just over a month. According to Reggie, he had found Bob's unresponsive body on Friday, 12th April. Slim located the papers from the 13th through to the 15th, and took them to a booth to scan through the side columns for any brief mentions of the incident.

He could find nothing at all that mentioned Bob Harker, but in a tiny corner column on page nine in one newspaper, the Southwest Morning News, he found the briefest of notes:

A Mr Reggie Bowles, of No. 124 Pier View was arrested this morning accused of wasting police time. He was later released without charge.

It was nothing, but it was the beginning of a trail. Slim went online, found a list of newspaper staff, and as was common these days, found that most had some kind of online presence. He sent a few messages, then left the library, wandering around for a while until he found a local café in which to wait.

It didn't take long. He was barely halfway through his first coffee when his old Nokia 6633 began to vibrate with an unknown number. Slim picked it up and pressed it to his ear.

'Yes?'

'Is that John Hardy?'

'Speaking.'

'Paul Williams, Southwest Morning News. I believe you sent me an enquiry about a police report?'

4

PAUL WILLIAMS WAS a junior news desk reporter, dealing with the kind of low interest stories that newspapers used to fill gaps between major stories and ads. A church prize. A stolen bicycle. Vandalism of a park gate. A broken-down tractor blocking a road. He told Slim that he received a daily email from the police detailing minor events, but instead of the trail ending there, he was able to give Slim a contact name in the local police.

An hour later, Slim found himself waiting near the entrance to the Grand Pier for Karen Tasker, a detective in the local police. While he had been expecting an officer in uniform to show up in an official car, he got something of a surprise when a woman walking a small Pomeranian dog hailed him as the dog nosed at the promenade wall.

'Slim, is it?'

'That's what some people call me, yes.'

She was about forty, shorter than him, still pretty but with a weathered look that he knew well. Police work aged people prematurely, the weight of what you saw like a leaking pipe, draining the years away. On a blustery afternoon, she had her hands stuffed into the pockets of a long coat that hung to her ankles, a woolly hat pressing shoulder-length light brown hair against her face.

'The famous Slim Hardy. I never thought I'd see you in our neck of the woods. You're at least two feet shorter than I expected.'

'You flatter me, Detective.'

'Please call me Karen. I'm off duty. No way I could be wasting police money on this. When I heard from you, I thought it was someone having a laugh.'

'You're still flattering me. To be honest, I'm not sure why I'm here, either. A man who might or might not be crazy accosted me at a book signing to insist I listen to a story about a dead man whose body had disappeared.'

Karen nodded. 'I was on the scene. I wish I could tell you that you're at the start of something, but sadly I can't. Reggie Bowles—the man who contacted you, I presume—is known to us. In layman's terms, you could say he's delusional, a fantasist. Sadly, a medicated one, not given the proper care. He shouldn't be allowed out and about without supervision, but he's not deemed a danger to the public so Social Services let it go.'

'So what he claimed was just an invented story?'

'I have no doubt that elements of it were true. He might well have seen his friend Bob Harker down there under the pier. What we've also established is that Bob Harker wasn't dead; at some point he must have got up and gone home. A couple of junior officers were sent round to his address, where they made contact with Bob and confirmed that he was alive and well.'

'So Reggie was mistaken?'

'Yes. He was adamant that Bob Harker's body had been removed; however, we've found that to not be the case.'

'Why say it in the first place?'

'As I said, he's a fantasist.'

'Reggie told me that the body was cold, that Bob's eyes were open, that there was a dark stain on his clothes that suggested blood, maybe a stab wound of some kind.'

Karen cocked her head. 'If Reggie saw Bob at all, it's worth remembering that Bob was a performer by trade. It could have been an act. By all accounts, Bob wasn't the most mentally stable of people either.'

'Did your officers have confirmation from Bob about that?'

Karen shook her head. 'They merely had to establish that he was alive and well.'

'They spoke to him?'

'According to their report, he refused to answer the door but spoke to them through it. They made a positive identification through the letterbox.'

Even though Karen spoke as though the case were done and dusted, Slim couldn't shake off a lingering suspicion that something was amiss. It sounded like shoddy police work, the kind undertaken by overworked officers with a pressing need to be somewhere else.

'Would there be any objection if I paid Bob a visit myself?'

'It's a free country, Slim. None at all.'

5

IT WAS a cold and windy day when Slim walked up Bolton Street on the town's outskirts to Number 14, the house belonging to Bob Harker.

Before he'd even reached the front gate, the evidence of neglect was everywhere: an unkempt, rubbish-strewn garden, tiles loose along the top of the wall, mouldy drapes pressed against dirty windows. Donald Lane had found him the address, and now, as Slim looked up and down the empty street, a couple of boarded-up houses and one wheel-less car giving a general impression of the neighbourhood, he wondered how a Punch and Judy man had ended up living here. Or, he considered, possibly dying.

The house, with its peeling paint and grimy windows, looked abandoned. As Slim reached for the door handle he thought better of it, instead taking a cloth from his pocket.

The handle turned, and the door, unlocked, gave a little before jamming on something lying inside. Slim's nerves jangled, and he wondered if he had already found Bob, but there was no giveaway smell of decomposition, nothing in fact except the damp scent of wet paper. A further nudge confirmed his suspicion that the door was blocked by a considerable heap of unsorted post.

Slim leaned on the door, trying to create a space large enough to slip inside. He had almost made it when he caught movement in the reflection from a downstairs window: someone in the street behind him.

He turned, offering an apologetic grin to the woman standing in the middle of the street. Wild-haired and portly, she looked too old to be the mother of the infant she carried in her arms, unless age had been very unkind indeed. A blouse was missing a top button; a knee-length skirt left thick, veiny calves exposed. On her feet she wore a pair of fluffy pink slippers, although the toe of one was crusted with what could have been animal or child vomit.

'I suppose you're not trying to break in or you'd have gone round the back,' she said in a rasping voice that suggested her obvious poverty still allowed enough money for cigarettes. 'Not a relative, are you? Young enough to be Bob's son, but he never had one, far as I know.'

'I'm a friend of a friend,' Slim said. 'My friend is worried because he's not seen Bob for some time. Since I said I would be passing, he asked me to stop by.'

'He in there?'

'I haven't established that yet.'

'Not seen him in a while, although the pigs were round the other night, knocking on the door.'

Slim immediately labelled her as a local know-all.

'Did he answer?'

The woman gave the best shrug she could while strad-dled with an infant.

'I suppose. They left soon after.'

'You didn't see him? They didn't go inside?'

'No. Not that I saw, but it's not like I have all evening to be spying on the neighbours, you know.'

Slim smiled. 'Of course not. Listen. Would it be possible to leave you my number? I'd really like to know if Bob shows up.'

'Sure.' She somehow pulled an expensive smartphone out of her pocket without dropping either it or the child. Slim caught a glimpse of the child in her arms, along with two others of a similar age, on the phone's lock screen before she opened it and scrolled to the phone book.

Slim gave her his number, noticing the odd look she gave his ancient Nokia.

'What's your name?'

'Ah … Mike. Mike Lewis. I'm a BBC researcher. We're planning a documentary about traditional seaside entertainment.'

'I thought you were a friend of a friend?'

Slim gave a sheepish shrug, both annoyed at himself for such an obvious slip up and aware at the same time that a little fallibility might make him more appealing to her.

'I can't keep anything from you, can I?' he said. 'I just heard Bob was a private man away from his work. If he knew I was coming, he might not answer the door.'

The woman chuckled. 'It's like being part of a conspiracy.'

Slim forced a smile. 'Quite. I'd really like to know if you see him. Or indeed if anyone else shows up. We have a … budget for local assistance.'

'Do you now? Well, I'll be sure to keep an eye out.'

'Thank you. Can I take your name?'

'Cheryl Callow. C and C.'

Slim wasn't sure how else he might have spelled it, but he gave her a smile, thanked her again, then headed back to his car.

At the end of the street, a couple of teenagers who didn't look like the types to spend much time in school were standing a little too close to Slim's car for his liking, but as they were about to walk away, he called out to them.

'I'm looking for someone,' he said. 'Lives down there, number 14. He's not been seen in a while.' He pulled out his wallet, withdrew a couple of twenties, then held them out, along with a piece of card, blank other than his number, scrawled in black ink. You know anyone round here who might have anything to say, ask them to ring me. The name is Slim.'

One of the boys snorted with laughter. The other just stared at Slim as he set the money and the card down on the pavement, then climbed into his car and drove away.

6

'NOT SEEN HIM IN A WHILE, but you know, not the best weather for it.' The man adjusted his company cap in the wind, as though to emphasise his point. Pier Cruises. A sturdy, rectangular boat bobbed in the swell, but with no one waiting to board, it looked unlikely there would be cruises happening in today's challenging conditions. 'Set up like he's got, can't be rewarding carrying it around when there's no one about.'

'Do you talk to him much?'

The man shrugged. 'I nod hello, you know, just to be polite. Maybe mention the weather. He's not all that talkative.'

'For an entertainer?'

The man shook his head. 'Bob's a bit funny like. Do you know what I mean?' The man scratched his beard, shifting from foot to foot as though trying to think of the right words. 'Like, he's a character.' He shrugged again. 'At least I think so. Like, all the time.'

'So he's not the easiest person to talk to?'

'Well, I don't know. But I'd prefer to not see him than see him, if you know what I mean.'

'Is there anyone who might know him better?'

The man frowned, and Slim waited for him to shake his head. Then, almost as though he was having a light-bulb moment, he looked up, eyes bright.

'You could try the little theatre in the Grand Pier there. Being in the same industry, I'd hazard a guess they know of him at least.'

'There's a theatre inside the pier?'

'Yes, in behind all the amusement arcades and the ice cream shops. Not all that big. Mostly just does local productions and the panto at Christmas.'

'Thanks, I'll go and have a word.'

The wind buffeted him as he walked up the pier, causing him at times to hold onto the rail for support. To his surprise however, the Grand Pier was open, an old man in a duffel coat sat in a ticket booth waving away his offer to buy an entry ticket and pointing at the open gate.

Inside, beneath a towering steel roof, the amusement area was a sensory overload of noise and colour: arcade games, immersive attractions and miniature fairground rides bumped shoulders in a cacophony of rattles and bleeps, with enough flickering lights to make Slim squint. He gave it all a distasteful scowl as he made his way through the maze of claw machine games, shoot-'em-up booths, dance simulators and others he had never seen before. At either side were stairs and lifts to a second floor where he found food vendors and shops bulging with tat and gaudy junk. He passed a children's soft play area, a carousel, a hall of mirrors, a room of trampolines. Much of it was retro, threadbare. Stains on the heavily trodden floor showed where old machines had been replaced.

He went up the stairs again to a balcony level. Luminous plastic chairs poorly matched with nearby tables crowded a viewing space; a café counter offered unappealing calorie-laden junk food. Slim glared at a peeling laminate of a chest-sized coffee cup and wished he'd brought a flask.

To its saving grace, with the exception of a handful of staff wandering about or standing bored behind counters, the place was nearly empty. A group of foreign tourists sat around a table, their smiles more sarcastic than entertained. Three truanting schoolboys nudged a penny pusher machine with their knees, then scattered as an alarm fought to be heard over the background noise. An old man in a duffel coat turned pages in a newspaper that carried yesterday's headlines.

Slim found the theatre at the back of the pier building, nestled beneath steel girders beside a set of stairs leading to a 'romantic view' outdoor balcony. Remembering the wind, Slim doubted the promise would be seen through, so the padded door beneath a sign that read *Argo's Theatre of Wonders* was a preferable choice.

The door opened with a creak of leather padding and revealed a ticket counter inside a cramped reception, the walls adorned with peeling posters of old productions overlaying one another. The current show, a sea shanty tale of pirates, held a prominent position next to the ticket window. A portable popcorn machine that looked in need of a clean stood beside a rack of snacks and sweets. A drinks machine occupied a shelf behind the ticket booth, next to a stack of flyers, still wrapped in plastic.

The door Slim presumed was the entrance to the theatre was off to the right. The only other door besides the one he had entered through was behind the counter to the left. A plastic sign labelled it as PRIVATE.

He walked up to the counter and peered over the top.

Lino replaced the lobby carpet, and needed a clean. A stack of boxes, the top one open to reveal more flyers, left little room for movement.

'Excuse me? Is there anyone here?'

A sharp thump came from behind the door, followed by the scraping of a moving chair. Slim took a step back as the door opened and a man peered out. Unshaven and with too much hair, a large mole on his left cheek and eyebrows that looked manicured, the man looked like an out-of-work magician. He wore a dress shirt beneath a blue sweatshirt that bulged at the throat from a hidden tie.

'I'm sorry, we're closed,' he said, with a little more terseness than Slim felt he deserved. 'Didn't Fiona lock the door on her way out? If it's a toilet you're after, there's one further around, next to the café.'

'No, it's not that.'

'If you're after tickets, we're only running the Saturday shows at the moment, and until the end of May you can probably buy them on the door.'

'Actually, it's not about that.' He leaned forward, getting a better look at the flyers on the counter. Punch 'n' Judy: A perfect fairy tale. A picture of the two main characters inside a big red heart. One of them carrying a hammer. 'In fact, I'm here looking for information. I'm trying to locate a man called Bob Harker. I've heard he's a local entertainer, but he hasn't been seen in a while.'

The man's smile dropped. 'What do you want to find *him* for?'

7

MARIUS PAINTER STIRRED a cup of weak tea and shifted uncomfortably on the plastic chair. 'God, they make even less effort out of season. It astonishes me sometimes that anyone comes here at all.'

'You've been here long?'

'Seven years. The lease is for ten. Not sure I'll renew. Other vendors have seen their leaseholds double. Pricing us out into the sea. So, what is it you're after Bob Harker for?'

Slim glanced at Marius then made a show of sipping the tepid, lukewarm coffee, letting the pause linger. It was too early to harbour any suspicions but Marius had already displayed several signs prevalent, in Slim's experience, in guilty parties. Perhaps Slim, in his faded wax coat, old walking boots, and with a couple of days of unchecked stubble, had the look of an undercover detective. Or perhaps Marius was simply holding on to a secret he subconsciously wanted to get off his chest.

Eager to accept Slim's offer of a drink in the café, he had rattled off a brief personal history almost before they had found a table. A failed actor born to an Italian mother and a British father, he had led a nomadic life around the UK before coming across the open lease to a small theatre in the dilapidated pier. Sensing perhaps an opportunity to make up for his failed career, he took up the lease then used the theatre to host local as well as travelling theatre groups, including some in which he had small parts of his own.

'The theatre seats only a hundred,' he told Slim. 'It's an intimate space where patrons can get up close to the productions. We've had one or two famous people come through, some on the way up, others on the way down. There's nothing like seeing an old thespian so close you can feel the warmth of his breath.' His smile dropped. 'Unfortunately, in a place like this, certain … tropes are expected.'

'Like the sea shanties?'

Marius wrinkled a nose that was slightly crooked. Like Slim's own, it might once have been broken.

'A place like this attracts a certain crowd,' Marius said. 'You have to cater for the kids, the Saturday drunks, the tasteless. For lovers of real art … there's not much to be found.'

'You sound a little bitter.'

Marius shrugged. 'Have you ever been married?'

Slim frowned at the question. For a moment he experienced an uncomfortable flood of memories; then with a shiver he shrugged them off.

'Briefly. A long time ago.'

'I never have. I came close a couple of times, but I saw the writing on the wall before it was even written, so to speak, and I backed out. With the theatre, I never saw it, but it turned out how I imagined a marriage would be in time. Endless routine. Contentment, but little true happiness.' He leaned forward, and for a moment Slim suspected he was adopting a role from one of his productions. 'Disappointing.'

'Is the pier open all year round?' Slim asked, wanting to encourage Marius before he launched into some Shakespearean soliloquy.

'Yes, but for nine months of the year we don't see much business outside the weekend.'

'It must be hard to stay afloat.'

'I just about break even,' Marius said. 'A decent summer can fill the coffers, if you know what I mean. And the Christmas season is always a boost.'

'I suppose you'd find it hard if there was any competition,' Slim said.

'From an old man wandering the beach with a pop-up theatre? It's a different crowd.'

'So you have no knowledge of Bob Harker, or what might have happened to him?'

Marius gave a defiant smile, as though offering an obstacle for Slim to overcome. 'None, I'm afraid. He simply wasn't on my radar. You could speak to Fiona, though. She's a dog walker. She might have encountered him down on the beach at some point.'

'Thank you. If I could take her number, that would be great.'

'You said you were a friend of a friend ... someone's looking for Bob?'

'Reggie Bowles. I don't suppose you know him?'

Marius's smile dropped abruptly. 'Reggie,' he said, the name dripping with distaste. 'Yes, I know him. Sadly, I know him very well.'

8

THE WIND HAD DROPPED but the view of the beach and the sea remained bleak. Slim zipped his coat up to the neck and turned up the collar to keep the cold out. Even in May he could have made use of a decent scarf. From the Grand Pier's viewing balcony, he stared down at the grey-brown sand, at the barely distinguishable line between the sand and the sea, then followed the line of the promenade as it curved gently around the headland towards a promontory that blocked his view any further.

There, however, in the grey distance beyond the promontory, was a small island, connected to the land by a smaller pier, one that even at this distance looked in bad repair. Slim made a note to drive up and take a walk around, perhaps for no other reason than to look back on where he now stood and get a different perspective.

From his vantage point, he was unable to see where Reggie claimed to have found Bob's body, beneath the shadow of the pier where it met the promenade. He could, however, see the residential care home where Reggie lived and wondered whether it was worth paying the old man another visit.

After what Marius had said about Reggie, however, he wondered if there was much point. Perhaps it was time to cut his losses and leave before he was drawn in too deeply by the delusions of an old man. He had only Reggie's word that Bob was even dead, a word that was becoming less reliable as the days passed.

'Back in the early days, I started my own troupe,' Marius had said. 'I put an ad in the local paper and planned to put on my own performances. Now, you can't advertise for a theatre troupe without getting a few prima donnas, but once you get down to work, those only in it for the stardom tend to drop off. A couple of practice sessions in, Reggie showed up, claiming he used to be a jobbing actor.' Marius smiled. 'I used to be a jobbing actor, and I know how to pick one. It was clear straight away that the only stage he might ever have been near was one in a courthouse. He couldn't act, but worse, he couldn't take instructions. He was abrasive, difficult to work with, and pretty soon people started leaving. It came down to him or the group, so I told him he had to leave.'

'I'm guessing he didn't take it well.'

Marius shook his head. 'At first he seemed to, but then things started to go wrong. Someone sabotaged the electrics, so I had an outage during a show we were putting on. Then I had the police show up, saying there had been an accusation about my conduct towards minors in my theatre group. An anonymous tip-off. I was taken in for questioning, and while I was obviously let off, word got around. More people left the group. At this point there were only a handful left, and when one of them had her car vandalised during a rehearsal, I decided it wasn't worth it and shut the group down for good.'

Slim stared out at the grey water. The wind had got up again, riffling the water's surface, churning it up. He watched a fishing boat out on the horizon until it had gone out of sight beyond the distant pier, then headed back downstairs.

From the relative warmth of a seafront café he called Karen Tasker on a private number she had given him.

'I'm sorry if this is a bad time…'

'Just done breaking up a brawl at a bingo hall, believe it or not,' Karen said with a chirpiness that left Slim unsure whether or not she might be joking. 'How are you getting on?'

'I'm still here. I can't tell you much more than that. I'm yet to locate Bob Harker, however.'

'I can look into it a little more if you like,' Karen said. 'Unfortunately, we don't have the resources we'd like to chase up every query.'

'I appreciate that. I wondered if you had any further information on Reggie Bowles? Prior arrests, things like that.'

'I can run him through the computer. It might be a good idea to speak to his residential place. They might be able to tell you more.'

'Thanks. I'll try that.'

He did as she suggested, but as he had thought, they quoted patient privacy laws and refused to tell him anything about Reggie on the basis that Slim was neither a member of family nor a doctor involved with the facility.

Instead, Slim rang Don.

'Reggie, I presume short for Reginald,' Slim said, giving Don as much detail as he could. 'I'd guess he's between sixty and seventy.' He gave Don the care facility's address. 'Unfortunately, that's about all I have.'

'It's enough to get me started,' Don said. 'Give me a couple of days.'

Outside, the weather had turned savage, rain lashing the café windows, the wind rattling the door. Slim was reluctant to leave the café's warmth to undertake the mile walk back to his B&B at the far end of the seafront, and wished he'd brought the car. The girl behind the counter kept surreptitiously glancing up at the clock above the wind-worried door, aware it was already ten minutes past closing. Slim was just thinking about offering double the price for one last coffee when his phone rang.

'Yes?'

'Um, hello?'

'Who is this?'

'Is that, um, Mr Hardy? This is Fiona Wainwright. I work at the pier theatre. Sorry to bother you. My boss gave me your number.'

'Yes, I remember. Thanks for getting in touch. Is it about Bob Harker?'

'Yes, it is. That's right. I just wanted to let you know that I saw him the day before he disappeared.'

'You did?'

'Yes. I'm certain of it. And now that I think about it, I think he might have been in some kind of trouble.'

9

THE CAR PARK where Fiona had asked to meet Slim was little more than a lay-by viewing spot overlooking the storm-ravaged remains of the old pier Slim had seen from the beach. Despite the weather being even worse than the day before when Slim had received Fiona's unexpected call, a couple of hardy photographers leaned over large zoom-lens cameras, hoping to get something of value from the mist-shrouded ruin stretching out into the sea.

Slim was halfway through a flask cup of coffee when a little Fiesta pulled up alongside him and the passenger window was wound down.

Fiona was a narrow-faced woman with pencil-straight black hair flecked with grey and large round glasses perched on a nose that looked too steep to support them. Slim estimated her to be in her early fifties, a similar age to himself.

As he wound his window down she said, 'I apologise for keeping you waiting.' She smiled, seemingly amused. 'One of the cats got stuck behind the log rack.'

Refusing to allow himself to stereotype, Slim just shook

his head. 'I just arrived,' he said. 'What with this weather … I hope you got her out okay.'

'Him,' Fiona said, as though her cat's gender was of critical importance. 'He's a new one from the shelter. Struggling to adapt to a stable home. He's not getting along with the others.'

Others, plural. Slim allowed himself a smile. 'Thank you for coming.'

'I hope it wasn't inconvenient to ask you to meet me out here,' Fiona said. 'Look, why don't you jump inside? I can barely hear you over this wind.'

Slim assessed the likelihood of being kidnapped as low, then got out of his car and climbed into the passenger side of Fiona's car.

The car smelled of animals, overlaid with a cheap air freshener. Stickers for the RSPCA, Cats Protection, and more surprisingly, the National Trust clung to the insides of the windows, only slightly peeling. Slim noted a key chain hanging from the rear-view mirror: a posy of dried herbs, a little cat toy, a miniature Eiffel Tower, its colour faded. Fiona wore wellington boots over jeans. A raincoat bag was squeezed into the tray between the seats, beside a tatty box of tissues and a dog-eared Patricia Cornwell paperback.

'I didn't really think anything of what I saw until Marius mentioned your visit,' Fiona said. 'It was better weather that day and I was doing a little beachcombing. At this time of year, all kinds of stuff gets washed up.'

All Slim had seen washed up on the beaches was rubbish, but he knew the line about such things being another man's gold. Perhaps Fiona was some kind of artist.

'And you saw someone who resembled Bob Harker?'

'It was Bob Harker. He carried his theatre on his back. There was no mistaking him.'

'Were you known to each other?'

'Only to exchange pleasantries. I couldn't tell you anything about his life away from the beach. In fact, that was perhaps the strangest thing.'

'What was?'

'That he was up here.'

Slim stared out of the window. Fiona had left the engine running but turned off the wipers, so the old pier was just a dark smudge through the rain clattering against the glass.

'He was here?'

'Down by the gates to the old pier. Arguing with the security guard to let him in.'

'Tell me what happened from when you first saw him.'

'All right. I was down on the rocks below the pier, just looking around, you know. You can find all sorts of interesting things tangled up down there. There's not much sand up here so unless the weather's fine you don't see many people. I heard a commotion and went to see what was going on. And there was Bob, still with his theatre gear strapped to his back, getting irate with the security guard because he wasn't allowed onto the pier.'

'Did you hear anything that was said?'

Fiona gave her narrow chin a scratch as though considering whether to divulge the information. Slim couldn't help but wonder how many amateur sleuthing websites she was a member of.

'It's difficult to recall anything that made any sense. He sounded drunk or on something.'

'Anything you can remember could be helpful.'

'Well, I remember he clearly said, "the clock is ticking". Which made no sense at all because the only clock anyone knows about on the pier was the one in the little tower, and it was stolen last year.'

10

FIONA HAD LITTLE MORE to say that was anything other than speculation, but she did clearly remember the date, due to it being the same day as an appointment at the vet's for one of her cats, something that could be verifiable. Bringing up the date on her phone, she confirmed it was one day before Reggie had reported the discovery of Bob's body beneath the Grand Pier's walkway. Slim thanked her, wished her cats well, and waved her off from the car park entrance, the rain having eased to a gentle mizzle.

He had a trail now, something to work with. He would need to find and speak with the security guard, but as he headed back to his car he noticed one of the photographers still in situ, leaning over a tripod which held a large-lensed camera pointed towards the pier.

He wandered over and hailed the man, who stood up and gave him a smile.

'Any good shots today?'

The man, wearing a lightweight plastic raincoat over the top of another one, with a floppy fisherman's hat pulled over his head, had to be in his eighties. Sparse grey hair framed an ancient face, but when he smiled Slim felt the light of years of wonder beaming out. This man had been places, seen things. And he looked quite happy to tell Slim all about it as he reached for a flask at his feet.

'Some,' he said. 'The perfect shot out here is of the pier protruding out of the mist. Don't think I've quite got it today. The mist wasn't quite thick enough.'

'I imagine you get a few opportunities with this weather,' Slim said.

The man laughed. 'Without doubt. Are you much of a camera person?'

Slim shook his head. 'I have an interest, I suppose you could call it, in things like that.' He nodded towards the ruined pier. He could see now that the far end was built on top of a natural island rather than being entirely man-made like the Grand Pier. 'Places we've left behind.'

'You're a ruins explorer?'

Slim considered his response. 'More of a historian,' he said. 'Can you get out onto that pier?'

'Not without a lot of nerve, plus a little luck. It was sold again six months ago, making it privately owned. Allegedly the council offered it to both the National Trust and English Heritage, but neither of them wanted it. You can see why. There's not much left.'

'Why would a private owner want it?'

'Yet another supposed restoration project, I imagine. It closed to the public in the eighties, but it's changed hands a dozen times since then. Some developer off the back of a big windfall sees pound signs, picks it up for a low price. Then nothing happens.'

Slim chuckled. 'Writes it off as a tax break.'

The man nodded. 'I can see you're a man who knows money.'

'Only how to lose it.'

'That describes most of us, doesn't it?'

'Sadly so.'

'Are you looking to go out for a look around?'

Slim gave a nervous laugh. 'By the look of it, I doubt it's very wise. It looks set to fall into the sea.'

'I think it says something about my personality that I come out here when the sea is high in the hope of catching it in the act. It's withstood everything the sea could throw at it so far, however. Seriously, though, if you wanted a look, have a word with the man down there on guard. He might take you out if you slip him a four-pack.'

Slim grimaced at the idea of buying alcohol. His latest dry streak was six months long, and he was determined to keep to it this time. He was too old for the life of an alcoholic, functioning or not. Then again, he could remember telling himself the same thing years ago.

'I'd sooner go out there by boat,' he said. 'Is that an option?'

'On a calm day, for sure. They'd see you coming, however. Better to have a word with the guard down there. You never know.'

'I'll give it some thought.'

Slim started to walk away, but the man called to him. 'However, if you did fancy a boat trip, my son-in-law runs fishing trips. It's quiet this time of the year, if you know what I mean.' He reached into his pocket and pulled out a card. 'Here.'

Slim took the card, gave it a look, then put it into his pocket.

'Thanks.'

He left the man to his photography and headed down a set of steps to a crumbling promenade where the entrance to the pier was blocked by a tall, temporary construction fence. A couple of signs warned him of both danger and prosecution. Nearby, a transit van was parked at the end of a gravel road, the logo for a security firm on its side. Slim went over and tapped on the window. A burly shaved-headed man wearing a yellow hi-vis jacket sat up with a start. Slim caught a brief glimpse of a film playing on his phone before the man put it down on the passenger seat.

The window slid down. 'Yeah?'

'Sorry to bother you,' Slim said. 'I take it you're the guard for the pier over there?'

'Yeah. That's right.'

'Do you know who owns it now?'

'Nope. We just do security.'

'Would your boss know?'

The man shrugged as though Slim's questions got on his nerves.

'I suppose.'

'Do you have a number for him or her?'

The man shrugged again. 'Go on the website. It's on the side of the van.'

'Thanks … just out of interest, if I wanted to go out for a look around, how could I do that?'

'Mate, it's private property. Go out there and you're trespassing. If you're stupid enough to try it, I ain't gonna stop you, but I will call the police. Not like I care if you end up killing yourself, but I ain't getting blamed for it.'

'I see. Do you get many people going out there?'

'All the time. All these idiot ruins explorers. I've pulled a few off the fence myself, but once they're over the top, it's a police job. I ain't going out there.'

'I don't blame you.'

'The whole walkway is a death trap. The wood's rotten and buckled; the iron frame is rusting away. They should pull the whole thing down.' He gave Slim a rare smile. 'But I suppose if they did, I'd be out of a job.'

Slim nodded. 'I don't suppose you recall encountering an old man a few weeks ago who had a similar request? Perhaps wanting to get onto the pier?' He gave the man the date he had learnt from Fiona, but wished he had a picture of Bob.

'Nope. But there are three of us who work in shifts. I'll have a word with the other lads, see if anyone remembers anything.'

'Thanks.'

'You got a number?'

'Sorry, yes.' Thinking it might be a good moment to inject a little intrigue into the proceedings, he took a business card out of his pocket. As he pressed one curled corner flat, he scolded himself for not getting around to buying a case for them.

On one side it said John Hardy, Private Investigator. On the other, handwritten in biro, his phone number. He had never bothered with an address because he didn't stay anywhere for long, and the website he had once started had fallen out of use. Nevertheless, clients still managed to find him.

'Huh? This for real?'

'Yes,' Slim said. 'It is. I'm looking for the man who got into the altercation with one of your colleagues. You see, the day after he was seen here, he disappeared. In fact, it's quite possible it was the last time he was seen alive.'

The man sat up. 'I'll have a word with the boys.'

'Thanks. I appreciate it. I'm sorry to have disturbed you.'

'No probs.'

Slim left the man alone, wandering to the edge of the old promenade, from where he could look out at the treacherous stretch of the old pier. Reaching some three hundred yards out into the sea, the old walkway was buckled in places, rotten in others, completely missing in some areas. Many of the steel struts were bent or missing, some lying on the rocks below the pier or protruding from the sea, rusted into misshapen lumps. From here, however, he could see that its far end was indeed a natural island, built up with several stone structures, a couple of shorter piers extending out at right angles to the first.

Two piers: one a crumbling ruin, the other a hive of retro activity. How could Bob Harker be supposedly found dead beneath one the day after trying to force his way onto the other?

Slim reached into his coat pocket and withdrew a small pair of binoculars. He held them to his eyes and adjusted the focus. The mist had cleared enough to give him an unhindered view of the pier island. Few structures still remained, and those that did looked in poor repair: damaged, fire-stained, graffiti-covered. There in the middle, though, was a thin brick tower. Slim moved the binoculars up and down.

It looked like a clock tower, three times the height of a man. Perhaps the clock Bob had allegedly said was ticking? But where a clock face might have been, there was only a gaping hole.

11

SLIM DROVE past Bob's house a couple of times before parking further up the street and walking back. A week since his last visit, and nothing had outwardly changed. The grass looked a little longer. No one had cleaned the grime on the downstairs windows. A couple of letters poked out of the letterbox, bent out of shape. Slim walked up the path and leaned over, careful not to touch anything.

On the top was an unpaid water bill red reminder, dated two days ago.

To legitimise his presence, he knocked on the doors either side of Bob's terrace, planning to introduce himself as BBC researcher Mike Lewis. No one answered on the left, while on the right an old lady leaning on a walker peered at him then tapped the side of her head and shrugged. Instead, he headed across the street and knocked on Cheryl Callow's door. Unencumbered by children this time, she could only offer some self-serving but ultimately hollow speculation. She hadn't seen Bob return, and no one had come to the house since Slim's previous visit.

Disappointed but not dissuaded, he went around to the

alley at the terrace's rear. He found an abandoned milk crate to use to look over the rear wall into Bob's small yard, and to his surprise found a neat patio, as though Bob saved all his energy for the back garden while ignoring the front.

The suggestions of neglect were apparent, however, with grass beginning to peek out between paving slabs and around the ornamental plants in pots arranged on stepped racks. A small pond with a bubbling solar-powered fountain needed the leaf litter cleared, and a vegetable garden containing lines of carrot seedlings really needed weeding.

Slim looked around, hesitating just a moment before pulling himself up onto the wall and climbing over. Muscles long neglected pulled taut, and he felt something stretch in his shoulder as he landed.

Scowling as he massaged the back of his neck, searching with his fingertips for the muscle he had strained, Slim approached the back of the house. A tiny sun lounge, big enough for perhaps only a couple of chairs and a small table, was a later addition to the main house, looking a little out of place. A door opened directly onto a raised section of paved patio. Another door, entering the kitchen, opened out of the wall to the right, directly onto a concrete path that bordered the vegetable garden. A shed stood in a corner to Slim's right, the pond to the left. A tall wooden gate that opened into the alley he had entered from was padlocked shut.

Slim approached the house, wondering whether the sun lounge door or the kitchen would offer the easier access. For a few seconds as he stood by the sun lounge door, he wondered whether he ought to walk away, perhaps call Karen Tasker and encourage her to look further into Bob's disappearance, then gave a slight shake of the head.

They didn't care; no one did. Without a body, Bob was

just a statistic, one of the 170,000 people reported missing in the UK each year. Even discounting the false alarms, those found quickly, and those who returned of their own accord, there were just too many. Slim had heard it called a silent epidemic, and the police didn't have the resources to go off chasing ghosts. Those few brief minutes by the pier and the apathetic visit by the trainees who claimed a visible identification were the only police man-hours Bob's disappearance was going to get.

Slim pulled out a pack of disposable rubber gloves from his pocket, opened it, and pulled the gloves on. Then he reached for the handle of the sun lounge door.

To his surprise, it opened without resistance. At the sound of a wooden creaking, Slim squatted down and peered at the door handle. A fine hardwood frame, perhaps oak or mahogany, damaged around the lock by some kind of chisel.

Slim frowned, one hand pressed against his coat, feeling the thin sliver of metal that was his own often-used lock-pick. A far subtler instrument. Whoever had broken in here either had less experience of the art of breaking and entering or had been in something of a hurry.

His thoughts turned to the supposed identification of Bob Harker made by the police. Not Bob, but someone else, inside his home.

Slim hesitated. He was potentially entering a crime scene. He ought to call it in now, but would the police listen? Did they have the resources to spare? Would they send another trainee who'd shrug and walk away?

He nudged the door with his foot, widening the space to step inside. Despite the cool weather, the sun room was warm, the air dry, a little stale. A closed door led through into a small living room.

Slim took one slow, measured step at a time, careful not

to move or touch anything. His eyes scanned the small space: a tasteful pastel print hanging on the inside wall, a vase of dried flowers on a shelf, a wicker box of knitting, a couple of tatty romance novels on a small glass table, their covers sun-faded.

Slim reached into his pocket and took out a camera, photographing the room from the floor to the ceiling, then he moved on to the next room.

A small living room, one sofa and a reclining fake leather chair. A table where a TV had been, its absence marked by a dust-free rectangle, and indicative of thieves. Slim again photographed everything but touched nothing.

A small, boxy corridor with a kitchen to one side, simple pine-finished units, cottage-like. Here, a microwave-sized space offered more suspicion, but there were no open drawers, no obvious signs of a search for money or valuables. Slim paused long enough to photograph a wall calendar, a cork board. A few photographs on a mantelpiece, of Weston beach: a group of people standing in front of a pop-up theatre, another dog-eared sepia photograph of a smiling young boy standing on a pier, blurry buildings behind him. Feeling a need to leave as soon as possible, he decided to examine the contents later.

A downstairs toilet and shower room had wall bars and a seat inside. Slim frowned. There were more bars along the wall.

The room next to the kitchen was a workroom, benches and shelves lining the walls littered with objects that might have played a part in Bob's productions, or were lined up for future roles. One shelf held a line of tattered, well-used puppets, while on a tabletop in the centre were several half-finished dolls and props. The room smelled of resin and wood clippings, so strong that he pulled the door closed after he had finished taking photographs.

The porch showed signs of abandonment: a pile of uncollected post, a couple of coats that had fallen off a hook left lying on the floor. Shoes that had fallen out of a rack and not been replaced. Slim stared at them, aware of what they suggested, then took another photo.

He headed upstairs. Three doors. One, half open, revealed a small bathroom. The other two he guessed were bedrooms. The door to the first was ajar. A bed, taking up most of the room, unmade. A fly lying dead on top of crumpled bedsheets. The window faced the street, but the curtains were closed. The air musty and dry. A cupboard door, ill-fitting, had popped loose. Inside, jumpers, jeans, trousers and t-shirts were folded in uneven piles and squeezed into boxy shelves. A dresser behind the door had a box of creams and lotions: Savlon, E45, Sudocrem, a supermarket brand of athlete's foot cream for someone who spent their days trudging back and forth across a beach. As someone else whose legs walked a lot of miles, Slim felt a certain kinship with this man he'd never met.

An old acoustic guitar sat in a corner, its strings in need of changing. A hoover, its electrical cord wrapped around the handle, stood behind the door.

Slim backed out of the room, increasingly aware of a growing smell, and a strange hum, like a generator, that came from behind the other, closed door.

He reached out with gloved fingers, twisting the handle, pushing the door open enough to see inside.

The stench might have made him vomit if the sudden rush of flies hadn't induced a knee-jerk reaction. He dropped to the ground as the cloud passed over him, covering his nose with his sleeve as he looked inside.

The sun on the back of the house illuminated the room enough through the closed white curtains for Slim to see the skeletal remains lying on the bed. He frowned, then reached up and slammed the door closed.

The situation had changed. Heart racing, hands shaking from what he had seen, he went downstairs, propped open the back door, then took out his ancient Nokia and called Karen Tasker.

12

THE DOOR OPENED. Karen Tasker gave the officer sitting opposite Slim a grim smile and nodded. The officer went out while Karen took his seat. She looked at Slim and sighed.

'The good news is you're free to go, and thanks to your reputation, you're not likely to be charged with any of the minor misdemeanours that a lesser man might have been slapped with.' She gave him a glare that left him in no uncertain terms that she had gone into battle for him and won. 'The bad news is that you're requested to stay within the county for the next two weeks in case we need to question you further.'

'I'm sure I can find things to do.'

'Just stay away from Bob Harker's place while the forensics team do their job. You're not part of the investigation.'

'That wasn't Bob, was it? I saw enough to know that wasn't him.'

'I can't tell you anything more at this stage. A statement will be issued in due course.'

Slim nodded. The look in her eyes told him she would fill him in later when they were no longer being recorded.

'So I'm free to leave?'

'For now.'

'Thank you.' Slim stood up. 'I could really use a coffee … and a shower.'

Karen pulled a card from her pocket and slapped it down on the tabletop.

'Here's a number for a local taxi firm.'

~

SLIM WAS TOO SHAKEN by what he had seen to go back to the B&B and rest. He asked the taxi driver to drop him off on the promenade near the Grand Pier where a warm sun and a drop in the wind had tempted a few people out for ice creams. Slim sat on a bench and watched a kite flyer with no control crash their kite into the sand a couple of times, then, remembering he had to eat sometimes, bought a bag of chips from the shop by the pier's entrance.

The manager, Richard Hardberry, recognised him from their previous meeting.

'Mike, isn't it? Have you managed to get your documentary off the ground yet?'

Slim chuckled. 'I suppose you'd say we're still in development. In other words, no. I don't suppose you've seen Bob Harker since we last met?'

Richard shook his head. 'I'm afraid not.'

'Maybe he really has disappeared.'

Slim picked at a couple of chips, wondering if Richard would offer anything, but the man turned back to his fryer and began scooping glistening pieces of battered fish onto a metal rack. Slim turned and stared up the arc of the beach, where the air was just clear enough for him to make out the end of the old pier protruding beyond the headland.

'That out there,' he said, getting Richard's attention, 'is that another pier?'

Richard looked up. 'Oh, that? Yes, it is. You can see it today, can you? Usually it's a little too misty.' He put down a pair of tongs and came out of the booth through a side door, then shielded his eyes with a hand. 'Used to have good times out on that pier, back in the day.'

'You went there?'

'Mum and Dad used to take us up there as kids, before Mum pulled her disappearing act. Dad didn't like being around the Grand Pier because it was too much like being at work, so we'd always go up there.' He grinned. 'Then, when I was a teenager … it was a place you'd take girls, if you know what I mean. It was already on the way out, used to close at six o'clock. You could climb over the gate and sneak out there if you wanted to be alone.' He chuckled. 'At least that was one of the rumours going around school. The only time I ever went out there was with a couple of lads for a dare one night. We came across this homeless woman. Scared the hell out of us all. I'd love to know how quickly I sprinted back along the pier. Must have broken a few records.'

'What year would this have been?'

Richard frowned. 'Late eighties, I suppose. I moved away with Mum when I was seventeen, so that would have been … about eighty-five? I came back to take over the shop in the late nineties, and the pier was long closed by then. You'd probably have to talk to someone up at the town museum to find out specific dates, if you're that interested.'

'What was it like?'

'Oh, nothing special. It was already getting run-down,

even back when I was a kid. There were always sections roped off for repairs, and half the shops were shut. There's a second smaller pier off the island round the back which you can't see from here, and you could take boat tours from there, which was probably its main attraction. Otherwise, there were just a couple of small funfair rides, a little theatre and an amusement arcade. A café, I think. Mum and Dad would just sit and drink coffee and let us run around.'

'You said there was a theatre?'

'Yeah, a small one.'

'Do you remember any of the performances?'

'No, sorry. Too long ago. I was a pretty hyperactive kid; I doubt I would have sat down long enough to watch anything.'

'I just wondered if Bob Harker might have been involved.'

Richard shrugged. 'He might have been. I don't know.'

Slim had more questions, but a couple of customers had appeared so Richard went back into the booth to serve them. Slim took his chips down onto the beach then walked up to the sandy area below the struts of the pier where Bob Harker's body had supposedly been found.

Before long, news of the body he had discovered in Bob's house would get into the press. He probably had only a few hours before stories started to change.

Finishing his chips, he headed back up to the promenade to pay Reggie Bowles another visit.

13

SLIM WAS REQUIRED to give his name and wait downstairs for Reggie's approval. He didn't have to wait long; Reggie came stumping down the stairs, and after a brief frown as though he was trying to dig Slim's face out of his recent memory, invited Slim into a conservatory room with tables already set up with cutlery for dinner. As he moved a fork and knife rolled in a napkin to make space for his phone, Slim noted that they were plastic.

'Any news on Bob?' Reggie said immediately, then nodded at a self-service drinks table in the corner. 'They have tea, coffee, iced water.'

'Thank you. I'm afraid no news yet,' Slim said. 'I have been making a few enquiries. At the moment I'm still trying to establish some background. For example, I have found that Bob was in an altercation with a security guard the day before his disappearance.'

'Really? Where?'

'Up near the old pier. The derelict one.'

'Oh, right.'

'That doesn't surprise you?'

Reggie tugged at his ear. 'Bob was a wanderer. Especially on a quiet day.'

'Do you know why he might have wanted to get onto the pier?'

'No. Do you want a coffee?'

Reggie was already getting out of his seat before Slim could answer.

'All right, sure. Black, no sugar.'

'Great.'

Slim waited while Reggie went to the drinks table, casting nervous looks over his shoulder as though to reassure himself that Slim was still there. Slim again began to wonder if perhaps Reggie was some extravagant fantasist taking him for a ride. After all, there was a decomposing body in Bob's upstairs bedroom. When the surrounding circumstances were fully established, it could mean anything. Bob could have gone on the run. He might now be a murderer.

Reggie returned with two drinks: a coffee for Slim and a tea for himself so thick with sugar that Reggie's spoon scraped against undissolved granules as he stirred.

'Did Bob ever talk to you about family? A wife, children?'

Reggie frowned as he peered through the window, where it had started to rain again. 'Not that I ... he mentioned a sister once. Just in passing, like. Said he was going up to visit her for ... for Christmas. That was it. I suppose it must have been last year?'

'Did he ever mention her name or whereabouts she lived?'

'Oh no, nothing like that.'

Slim forced a smile. 'It's all right. I'll ask around.'

He sipped his coffee, wondering if he had made a mistake in coming here. Reggie continued to stare out of the window, his spoon slowly revolving through the sugar granules at the bottom of his cup. Slim closed his eyes and briefly imagined the sea moving over shingle, knocking the stones together.

'And you don't know why he might have been up at the old pier?'

'Oh, no.'

'Did you ever go up there?'

Reggie looked away from the window suddenly, fixing Slim with a gaze so hard it was unnerving. The shattered remnants of old memories swirled in those eyes, slowly piecing back together.

'No, no,' Reggie said, looking away again. 'Not since … not in a long time.' He finally stopped stirring, dropping his spoon on the tabletop, and began scratching furiously at the back of his right hand. Slim watched him, noticing how the knuckles looked lumpy, misshapen.

'Reggie, are you all right?'

Reggie shook his head back and forth and began to moan as his left hand scratched the back of his right with greater intent until spots of blood appeared on the skin.

'Reggie?' Slim reached out and put a hand over Reggie's. The scratching immediately ceased and Reggie looked up as though broken from a trance. 'Reggie, it's all right.'

Reggie stared at Slim, then looked down at the scratches on his hand. 'Oh dear,' he said. 'Oh dear.'

Slim handed him a serviette and Reggie dabbed at the spots of blood.

'I'm sorry if I upset you with my questions. It wasn't my intention. I'm just trying to find out what happened to Bob.'

'Bob is dead,' Reggie said. 'I saw his body. He was cold. They took him, hid him, covered it up.'

'Who did? And why? Can you think of anyone who might have disliked Bob enough to hurt him?'

Reggie stared at the tabletop, frowning.

'There was this one man,' he said at last. 'But I don't remember his name.'

14

SLIM LEANED against the buttress wall by the end of the pier and looked along the line of houses and other seafront properties. Most were residential homes or B&Bs. There were a couple of businesses—a solicitor a little further along and an accountant almost directly opposite, but none had what he was looking for: security cameras which might have been able to prove that Bob was in the vicinity of the pier when Reggie claimed to have found his body.

The biggest irony was that a council-owned camera stood on a pole across the street and was trained on the pier entrance. On examining it, however, Slim had found it so crusted with salt and seabird faeces that it no longer offered any visibility. Upon making a call to the council, a work van had arrived to clean it up, but for Slim it was too little, too late.

Almost opposite the pier entrance was a street curving away through shops which eventually led to a town square. On the left corner as Slim stood with the sea at his back was a doctor's surgery.

A camera was fixed to the wall above the entrance. Its

angle was such that it might just have a view of the steps beside the pier which led down onto the beach.

The set of steps was the closest to where Reggie claimed to have seen Bob's body. Slim had two initial tasks; first to ascertain whether Bob had been anywhere near the spot where Reggie claimed he had died, and secondly whether he had later moved, either of his own accord or not.

He called Karen Tasker.

'Slim. Hi.' She sounded frustrated, tired of hearing from him.

'Karen, I've found a camera that might potentially show Bob's movements—'

'This is a police investigation, Slim,' she said with a tired sigh. 'You have to take a step back.'

'This is to do with his disappearance, not what was found.'

'Let it go, please. I told you; I'll call you when we have any official news.'

'Karen—'

The line went dead. Slim stared at his phone in frustration for a moment before dialling another number.

'Don, it's me.'

'What can I do for you, Slim?'

'That man, Bob Harker, I heard a rumour that he had a sister. If she's alive, I need to find her.' He hesitated for a moment, then added, 'There was a body in his house. Long dead, by the look of things. The police are still trying to figure out who it could be.'

'I'll have a look.'

'Thanks, I appreciate it. By the way, can you have another look into Reggie Bowles? I'm wondering how far their connection might go back.'

'Sure. Give me a day or two.'

Slim hung up and slipped the phone back into his pocket. He crossed the street, looking for other cameras, but none had a suitable view of the promenade or the pier entrance. He made a note of other nearby cameras in case he needed to trace a route, then retreated to a café as rain started to fall. There, he unfolded a map of the local area and began to calculate how Bob might have made his way down to the beach each day. From his house it was two miles as the crow flew, likely significantly further by way of the jumble of streets behind the seafront.

Bob, according to everyone Slim had spoken to, carried his livelihood on his back, something that even if lightweight and fold-up would still amount to a significant weight, plus perhaps an awkward size. He apparently had no car, so perhaps he caught a bus each day. Slim waved over the barista and asked for a local bus timetable. Then, using his map, he traced the lines of bus routes, checked times, and established a couple which Bob might have used.

An hour later, Slim found himself outside the office of the local bus company which managed the routes Bob might have used. A kindly receptionist stared through thick spectacles at a staff roster chart, then announced that the route was most often driven by Tim or Jenny.

Tim was out on a route, but Jenny happened to be across the yard in a cabin the receptionist rather generously referred to as the staff lounge. Looking pleased to get out from behind her desk, the receptionist led Slim across the yard and introduced him to Jenny Hodgson, who was in the process of making coffee and was happy to make a second for Slim.

Shaven-headed and with tattoos around her neck, she came across as rather fearsome, but when she spoke she had a joviality which put Slim immediately at ease.

'Bob? Oh, I remember him,' she said, passing Slim a paper cup. 'I always helped him with his gear. I didn't get these shoulders from press-ups alone, you know.' She grinned and flexed a bicep through her shirt for emphasis.

'I understand that he carried everything on his back,' Slim said.

'Oh, he did. I used to help him get the straps on when he got off. He looked like a tortoise staggering up the street. It wasn't all that heavy and the way it all folded up and packed away was quite clever, but it was most certainly awkward and I imagine if you had to walk far, it would have started to weigh you down.'

'Did you talk to him much?'

'A few pleasantries, not much else. The same with most of the customers.'

'Do you remember the last time you saw him?'

Jenny shrugged. 'A month ago. A little more maybe. He wasn't all that regular, particularly during low season or when the weather was poor. Sometimes I wouldn't see him for a couple of weeks. I heard he had gone missing, but it wasn't like you could set your watch by him.'

Just at that moment the cabin door opened and a young man walked in. Jenny waved him over, introducing him as Tim Fernby. He looked fresh out of school, barely old enough to drive, and greeted Slim with a cheerful smile and a firm handshake.

'You're a private investigator?' he said. 'Like on the telly?'

'It's not as exciting as it looks,' Slim said. 'But all the walking keeps you fit.'

'I bet it's more exciting than driving a bus,' he said. 'Although we had a punch-up on the ten-thirty last Friday. Six girls. Full on handbags swinging. Absolute chaos. This young lad got on and it seemed he'd been seeing two of them without either of them knowing.' He grinned. 'I suppose it can be a little exciting sometimes.'

'He's looking for Bob Harker,' Jenny said. 'The Punch and Judy man.'

'Oh, him. Not seen him in ages. I heard he'd gone missing, just thought he might have gone on holiday somewhere a bit warmer.'

'The last known sighting of him was on Friday the 12th of April,' Slim said. 'Roughly four p.m.' He recalled what he'd heard about Reggie. 'That's unconfirmed, however. I have a more reliable sighting of him on Thursday the 11th. I don't suppose you remember seeing him on either of those days?'

Tim frowned. 'I'd have to check the roster because I can't remember exactly what date it was, but I do remember the last time I saw him.'

'Why was that?' Slim asked.

'Because he had someone with him.'

15

LIKE MANY MODERN COMPANIES, finding an actual physical address for Johnson Security proved more of a chore than Slim would have liked. With its presence predominantly online, he was reduced to searching through the fine print which eventually revealed an office address in Bristol. Aware he was pushing the limits of his police restriction, he called Karen to inform her, but she just told him to keep his phone switched on.

He caught a train, feeling a sense of relief at getting away from the grey seaside town for a while. The endless expanses of open sand had caused him to crave crowded streets and narrow buildings, bustling crowds of people, the sound of cars over the rustling of the wind and the crash of waves.

Bristol, a place he hadn't been in some years, was as he remembered it, a city of colour and clutter, vibrant with its youthful population and its ever-changing selection of shops.

Slim found Johnson Security on a letterbox outside an office building at the end of a narrow side street. Several other companies occupied the same building. He pressed a buzzer and was let in to a glassy atrium. Two floors up in the lift, he emerged at a reception desk fronting a tiny office where two middle-aged women were standing by a window, drinking tea. One of them broke away to speak to him.

'This is Johnson Security?' Slim asked.

'It is,' said the woman, whose name tag introduced her as Madeline. 'Are you looking to hire some protection?'

Slim glanced at the other lady and smiled, trying to muster a little charm. 'I feel safer already,' he said.

The women shared a chuckle. Slim felt a moment of pride that he could still make women laugh; then he remembered why he was there.

'I'm trying to track down one of your employees,' he said. 'Your website wasn't exactly customer friendly.'

'Oh, that's how they do it these days, isn't it?' Madeline said, turning to the other woman, who was just close enough that Slim could make out the name Frieda on her name tag. 'It's all automated. Saves money. That's all people care about these days, isn't it?'

'My name is John Hardy,' Slim said. 'But most people call me Slim. It's a … long story. I'm a private investigator. I'm looking into the disappearance of a man whose last known sighting was in an altercation with one of your guards.'

'You don't think he was involved in this man's disappearance?'

'Not at all. I just want to know what was said. It might give me a clue as to what happened to the man in question.'

Slim gave the two women as many details as he could. Madeline went to a computer. Frieda leaned over her, offering help. Slim waited as they pulled up a staff roster.

'All right, that was at the Weston North Pier, right? Customer was J&L Development Ltd, assigned officers were Tony and Matt … around lunchtime, you said? That would have been Matt. Matt Owens.'

'Can I get a number for him?'

'You're not a police officer, are you?' Frieda said.

'No, no I'm not.'

The two women looked at each other. 'We'd best call him on your behalf,' Madeline said. 'We employ a certain … type of people.'

Slim nodded, understanding. 'He's an ex-offender?'

'Ah … yes.'

'Don't worry. You're looking at another. I understand how people sometimes make mistakes.'

The two women glanced at each other. 'What did you … er … do?' Madeline said.

Slim felt his cheeks burn with shame, but part of survival came from facing up to one's mistakes, and most— but not all—of his life's darkest times had been companions to drive him forward.

'Breaking and entering, common assault, DUI, affray…' He counted on his fingers. 'Drunk and disorderly … and manslaughter.' He sighed. 'There were probably others.' He forced a smile as he looked up. 'Are you hiring?'

The two women were staring at him. 'I can get you an application form,' Frieda said, then glanced at Madeline. The two women exchanged an empty chuckle.

'I only want to know what Matt remembers,' Slim said.

'I'll give him a call,' Madeline said, picking up a landline phone and brandishing it like a weapon.

～

MATT OWENS LIVED LOCALLY, and agreed to meet Slim in

a city centre coffee shop. As Slim might have expected for a security guard, he had a tough look about him, a tattoo beside one eye, a scar beside the other, hard lines across his face. He shook Slim's hand with gnarled, rough fingers, his grip iron hard. When he smiled, though, Slim sensed a lifetime of regret behind his eyes. He understood. He rarely used mirrors through the fear of seeing the same in his own.

'Am I in trouble?' Matt said, as soon as their pleasantries were over. 'Like, I need this job.'

Slim shook his head. 'It's only information that I'm after. I assume the lady at your company told you what I told her. I was contacted by a friend of the missing man. The last known sighting I have of him is being in an altercation with you about getting on to the old pier.'

Matt looked down. 'I remember. Crazy old fool. I told him to get lost.'

'What did he say?'

'He was rambling, like. When I first saw him coming up the road, I thought he was one of them tramps, you know, the cardboard city types, carrying all his gear. He was old, like eighty-odd, looked out of his mind. Eyes all over the place, mouth dribbling like he had rabies or whatever. I just wanted him to walk past; then when he came over, I thought I'd flip him a quid, whatever, and tell him to get lost.'

'He approached you?'

'Yeah, just had me hand in me pocket for a coin when he starts on about opening the gate.'

'The security gate?'

'Yeah. The one that blocks the old pier. Got a padlock on it.'

'He wanted you to open it for him?'

'Yeah. He says, "I have to go out there. I forgot something. Time's running out." Something like that. And I said you can forget it. I ain't opening that gate. And he tries to grab me, and I'm like, I can't smack an old man, but he's asking for it, you know.'

'What are you supposed to do in such circumstances?'

Matt sighed. 'There's a whole rule book, isn't there? De-escalate. Call it in to the office, or the police if necessary. Wait for backup.'

'And did you?'

Matt shifted, looking uncomfortable. He scratched at his chin. 'Am I in trouble?'

'No, not at all.'

'Are you sure? Look, I've been trying to make this job work, but sometimes … it's like the old ways, isn't it?'

Slim leaned forward. 'I've been inside too,' he said. 'I know how it works. I'm also an alcoholic. I've been dry nearly a year, but I'm only ever one drink away.'

He hoped a shared state of despondency might allow Matt to trust him. Matt nodded. He glanced around the coffee shop, then looked back at Slim.

'I told him I was going for a cig,' he said. 'Round the back of the van. I said, I'll be gone ten minutes, and when I get back, you'd better be gone, or there'll be trouble. He'd unnerved me a bit, so I was a little longer, maybe fifteen minutes, twenty. And when I came back, he was gone.'

Matt shook his head back and forth again, grimacing, dealing with personal pain.

'What happened, Matt?'

'The gate was open. I'd swear on my life that it was padlocked shut, but it was open, pulled back a foot or two.'

'And what about the man? Was he down on the old pier?'

'Don't have a clue. There was no sign of him. No sign of him at all.'

16

J&L Development Ltd. It had almost slipped by unnoticed during his conversation with Madeline and Frieda, but as his leads began to mount up, Slim decided it was worth taking a step back to get a wider view.

Almost as elusive as Johnson Security, he found only a solitary website with little of interest. They had built a couple of apartment complexes in London. No phone number, the only contact email getting an automated reply thanking him for his query and promising a lengthier reply at a later date. And the location address, when he finally found it buried in the small print, was for an office building in Sacramento, California. Another search for the building itself simply said it was a modern building with several resident companies, and further office space available for rent.

If he wanted more information, he would probably have to put Don on the task, but he had overloaded his friend already.

He had taken Matt's contact details, but unless the security guard was lying, there wasn't much else Slim expected to learn from him. His information in itself was potentially game-changing, but the rest of the facts didn't fit. He considered that Reggie, clearly not sound in the mind, had been mistaken, perhaps to the extent to which pier he had found Bob's body under. Could he somehow have mistaken the newer Grand Pier for the older North Pier, his memory perhaps delayed, and could Bob's body still be lying beneath the rusting frame of the old pier?

Unlikely, but it was as good a theory as any that he had.

The North Pier was three miles by road from the new one, protruding into the Bristol Channel on the nub of a headland. While the Grand Pier sat amidst acres of open sand, the old pier was surrounded by rocky cliffs, a few narrow inlets the only places to walk, the current beneath its struts treacherous, especially at high tide. From a modern point of view, its location made no sense, but setting his mind back a hundred and fifty years to when it was first built, Slim could understand the reason for its construction a little more. In the 1870s, when the North Pier had been built—then, according to a display in a local history museum, simply called the Pleasure Pier—the beach didn't hold the same attraction that it later would. The views up and down the Bristol Channel would have appealed more, while the deeper water would have allowed larger boats to dock.

Slim stared at grainy black-and-white photographs of channel-crossing paddle steamers disgorging hordes of white-clad revellers onto the jetty that protruded out from the far end of the pier, a jetty that later photographs showed had long since been lost to the sea.

Other displays explained that the pier's extension out into the channel meant steamers could dock regardless of the channel's huge tidal range, which could leave miles of mudflats exposed at low tide. At one point more than ten thousand people per day were alighting from the steamers, prompting the council to build the first Grand Pier to entice customers closer to the town. The Pleasure Pier— later renamed as simply the North Pier—remained popular for some decades more until the decline in steamer traffic, mostly caused by the rise in bus and private car travel in the post-war years, came into effect.

Eventually, overshadowed by its larger and better located neighbour, it began to fall into decline. Visitor numbers fell away, businesses closed, and the pier shut for good at the end of the nineteen-eighties. By now privately owned, it changed hands every few years, forever the target of a potential renovation project that was so far yet to happen. J&L Development Ltd was the latest in a long line of companies that had planned—but so far failed to produce—the North Pier's phoenix-like rise from the sea.

Like an old motorboat, Slim's mind spluttered with ideas as he sat in the museum coffee shop, watching the saplings in the small museum garden exposed to the buffeting wind. It made most sense that Reggie was mistaken, that he had seen Bob's body beneath the old pier rather than the new, had suffered some kind of psychotic episode and given the wrong information to the police.

If Bob really had ventured out along the old pier like Matt had suggested, it was possible. With the currents in the channel, the body could have been dragged out to sea.

But what about the rest? What about Bob's desire to get on to the pier in the first place? What about the talk of the ticking clock? What about the man seen by Tim on the bus with Bob on the last day he was sighted? Could it be the same man Reggie claimed had disliked Bob?

Then of course, there was the elephant in the room.

The decomposing body he had himself found in Bob's upstairs bedroom.

The suspense was killing him. He pulled out his phone to call Karen Tasker, but before he could dial the number, the phone rang, showing another number he recognised.

He held the phone to his ear. 'Don?'

'How you doing, Slim? I got something. I don't know how important it'll be, but it's big.'

Slim's heart began to race. 'Go on.'

'It's about Reggie Bowles. All this time I've been looking for a Reginald, but that's not his real name. I went through some databases, specifically looking for people with a police record and a registered history of mental illness. Somewhere along the line, Reggie became short for Frederick. And Frederick Bowles has quite a history.'

'Frederick?'

'In 1995, Frederick Bowles was convicted of the second-degree murder of a Mr James Ackerman, a Bristol resident. During an altercation, Frederick stabbed him in the neck, and went on to stab him twenty-three times. He served eighteen years of a twenty-five-year sentence, and was released in 2013.'

Slim whistled through his teeth. 'Right.'

'Be careful, Slim. That man you're dealing with is a convicted murderer.'

17

Don's news left Slim struggling to think straight. He returned to the B&B, eating a sandwich in his room while he pored over his notes.

Reggie's—or Frederick's—unreliability had just risen to another level. Don had promised to unearth what he could of Reggie's criminal record—while adding J&L Development Ltd to his lengthy list of research subjects, but for now all he had given Slim was a name.

James "Jackie" Ackerman.

Slim could only offer the name a grim smile as he stared at where he had jotted it down on a piece of crumpled paper. Jackie Ackerman just sounded like some kind of gangster, and it only took Slim a quick search online to confirm his suspicions. Ackerman had been known to police, was a career criminal, and a known member of a local gang called the E-boys, who had run protection rackets, dealt drugs, sold on stolen cars, and all manner of other criminal activity through the 1990s. Slim could find no criminal cases relating to the gang since 2001, so the members had likely got old, died, been imprisoned or been assimilated into other gangs.

As he went further down his internet rabbit hole, he came across the name of a former member who now advocated against gang violence, doing talks in schools, running youth clubs to keep kids off the streets. Robert Tiller had a website email and a phone number, so Slim sent a message and left a voicemail.

Taking a walk up the street from his B&B, he breathed in the cool night air and tried to clear his head. At the end of the street was a small park through which a river meandered along a stone-walled channel. Slim sat down on a bench beneath a streetlight and stared at the reflection of the light on the glittering water. A car rushed past, its misfiring engine coughing smoke from the exhaust. The sudden blast of a twenty-year-old song followed by raucous laughter announced the opening of a pub door further up the street. A group of men laughed as they stumbled drunkenly along the road behind the park, oblivious to Slim's presence.

He felt like he was holding a handful of marbles in his hand. All of them might mean something, but none of them seemed to connect. Was Bob Harker actually dead? Who was the very dead woman in his house? Who had been with Bob on the bus? What was Reggie's real involvement? Had he really found a body or was he simply looking for attention?

Slim closed his eyes and leaned his head back. Nothing made any sense. There was certainly a crime—perhaps several crimes—but he felt like he was walking around in a circle, leaving a groove in the ground beneath his feet but getting nowhere at all.

And then his phone rang.

He pulled it out of his pocket and stared at the number.

Karen Tasker.

She sighed when he answered before she even said her name, as though it were a call she didn't want to make.

'Karen?'

'Slim. Sorry to call so late.'

He smiled. 'It's fine. I wasn't sleeping. Sometimes I don't.'

'Where are you? I'd prefer to talk to you face to face rather than over the phone.'

Slim looked around. 'I'm sitting in a park at the end of Cheltenham Forest Road. On a bench.'

'Perfect. I'll be there in half an hour.'

Slim smiled again. 'Bring a coat. It's not warm. And if you have the chance to pick me up a coffee … I'd appreciate it.'

18

'WE DON'T KNOW who she is,' Karen said, hands cupping around her takeaway coffee cup as she leaned against Slim to let him shelter her from some of the wind. 'Forensics have done what they can, conducting DNA tests, searching dental records, running a reconstruction of her face through the missing persons' database, but as of now we can't identify her.'

'She has no familial match to Bob?'

'None. They scraped his DNA from the house and ran tests. No match. Not even close.'

'And there's nothing in the house to identify her?'

'That's what we're doing now, but so far ... nothing.' Karen let out an exasperated growl. 'Who the hell is she and where the hell is he? Do you know anything that can help us, Slim?'

'You must have some information to work with.'

'It appears she had been dead for at least a month, maybe even more. There were advanced signs of decomposition, as I'm sure you're aware, but there wasn't much of her to begin with. She had been very frail, of advanced age. Our team estimates she was between eighty and a hundred years old.'

'Have you checked out Bob's family background? Could she have been an adoptive mother, something like that?'

'We're working on it. At the moment, we're combing his property, looking for anything that might give us a clue. There's no documentation, no post, not even medication labelled for anyone other than Bob.'

Piece by piece, she told him everything the police knew so far. The woman had been bedridden, frail, but early signs were that she had died from natural causes. There were no external wounds, no signs of mistreatment. In fact, it appeared Bob had cared for her well prior to her death. The upstairs bedroom contained a wheelchair, and the bathroom was equipped with rails and supports. They had found over-the-counter creams and ointments for dealing with bedsores and rashes, food supplements, particularly calcium and vitamin D, designed for the elderly. The bedroom had a television and a stack of unreturned library books as though Bob had done his best to keep his guest entertained. A chair beside the bed suggested Bob may even have been reading the books to her.

Another easy chair that faced the window overlooked the garden, and Slim remembered how neat and tidy the rear garden had been compared to the front, as though Bob had made a special effort to improve the aesthetics in the direction the old woman would have been looking.

'Something else,' Karen said. 'There was a UV blind over the bedroom window. Indications from the autopsy are that the woman may have suffered from extreme light sensitivity.'

'The house faces south, meaning that the front windows would have caught the sun,' Slim said. 'The rear garden would have received sun over the afternoon, but the back bedroom window would have been in the shade.'

Karen looked up at him, holding his eyes for several seconds. 'You're right,' she said at last.

'Which is why, if she was sensitive to light, she was in the back bedroom rather than the front. And why Bob made no effort with the front garden if he only kept the rear tidy for her benefit. Have you begun to canvass the area?'

Karen nodded. 'So far, no one knows anything. Bob kept himself to himself. He had no interactions with any of his neighbours beyond pleasantries. He attended no local events and no one ever went to his house. He was drawing a state pension and also had a small military pension—'

Slim frowned, remembering something Reggie had said during one of their early conversations. 'Wait. A military pension?'

Karen turned to look at him. 'We found documents in the property that confirm he spent a few years in the Royal Navy. He fought in the Falklands War. We found a South Atlantic Medal engraved with the name of Robert William Harker. Our missing man was a war veteran, and a decorated one at that.'

19

THE POLICE, according to Karen, who swore Slim to secrecy, were treating Bob's disappearance as suspicious only because he might be involved in the unidentified woman's death. They considered Bob might now be on the run and were concentrating their efforts on finding positive identifications at bus and train hubs. However, with the woman's death almost certainly due to natural causes, Bob was not considered a danger to the public.

'We're stretched thin dealing with social unrest and domestics,' Karen had told him. 'We just don't have the resources to mount a manhunt for someone whose only crime at this stage appears to be body abandonment. Blame the government, whatever, but it looks like we either need Bob Harker to reappear or for some stroke of luck in identifying the dead woman. It looks like he could have just taken her off the street, except that she matches no one of that age group who has been reported missing.'

Slim allowed himself a smile. 'So what I think you're saying is that you need my help?'

Karen's answer hadn't surprised him. The police

needed his help but they weren't prepared to acknowledge that they needed his help; he was no more than an anonymous informant. Still, Karen said that within reason there would be no attempt to block his investigation, and she would provide him with whatever information she could.

So far, that wasn't much. And as on past occasions when he had become involved with the police, his first impulse was to walk away. It wasn't that they would take any potential glory to be had in solving the case; he had always actively shunned such things. It was that he preferred to work with his own thoughts. The police acted too much like a family, talking over themselves. Family had done nothing for Slim other than make him resentful. He preferred to walk his own path.

At the moment, however, he had very little to work with other than the titbits the police were feeding him, like a rabbit stuck in a cage.

And he wanted to be free.

He had developed a liking for Karen Tasker over their few brief meetings. She had a taciturn style, like a foot soldier grudgingly driving forward, but had an obvious dependability coupled with a frustration at the reins her job had strung about her. She wanted to break free too, but while still chained, she had seen her chance through Slim.

He couldn't let her down.

He called the bus company. Yes, they had cameras on all of their buses; no, the police hadn't been in touch concerning Bob Harker's disappearance. Slim requested copies of the videos from the last day Bob had been seen riding the bus plus those from a week prior. He was told it would take a few days to find and copy the footage, provided it still existed. An internet search told him footage was only kept for either twelve, thirty or sixty days, depending on the company, but the person he had spoken to was unable to tell him without checking.

Tim, the driver on the last day Bob was known to have taken the bus, however, had been happy to meet Slim for coffee and give a fuller account of what he had seen.

'It always took him time to get on board because he had his pack with him,' Tim said, absently peering through a rain-smeared window at the dreary street outside. 'It was like an oversized rucksack, but it looked like he'd carried it through both world wars, the amount it was patched up. Honestly, there were more patches on it than original material, if you get what I mean. But, it was like part of his act; he was just like a kind of character. You couldn't mistake him for anything else because he looked like he'd stepped out of an Enid Blyton book or whatever. His clothes were all patchwork like a quilt, and he wore a floppy seaside hat with little woollen seagulls sewn to it.'

One evening, a few days into his investigation, Slim had spent a couple of hours searching through social media websites for publicly visible holiday photographs. After trawling for hours he had come across some posted by a family from Birmingham with the title "we met a real Punch and Judy man!!". In one of the photos, two children stood either side of a smiling old man with sun-ripened cheeks and tufts of grey hair pushing out from under a fedora-like hat. Two tatty woollen lumps he supposed could have signified seagulls leaned on either side of the crest. When he showed a printout of the picture to Tim, the young bus driver nodded.

'That's him. How I remember him, at least.'

'What do you mean?'

'That last time, he wasn't himself. He had a faraway look in his eyes. He smiled when he showed me his bus pass, but it wasn't the usual smile. You learn to pick your regular customers' moods. You can tell when something's up.'

'This person who was with Bob that day … can you describe him?'

'I didn't give him much of a look to be honest,' Tim said. 'I didn't realise they were together. He was much younger, wore a hoodie like a lot of the … how can I say this politely? Rougher kids. The type you don't engage with.' He shrugged. 'We're told to just take their ticket and smile, don't make eye contact, don't try to start a conversation.' He gave a bitter laugh. 'I must sound like such a snob. I'm only twenty-five.'

'Just give me what information you can.'

'Well, he wasn't trying to help Bob or anything, just stood there with his hands in his pockets, looking impatient. Only after they went up the aisle I saw them sit beside each other in the front seat, behind the space for pushchairs. I watched them in the mirror. The young guy was leaning over, saying something to Bob, but I don't know what.'

'And they got off together?'

'Yeah. Again, the young guy didn't help Bob at all, just stood with his hands in his pockets while Bob hauled his bag out of the luggage rack. I was about to get up and help when he managed to get it. Then the young man followed him off. As I pulled away, I saw them in the side mirror, walking up the street, the young guy leaning in.' Tim sighed. 'I kind of didn't think much of it at the time, but I didn't know that was the last time I'd see Bob, you know? Like I say, he wasn't there every day. I didn't even think about it for a week or so, then just thought he'd gone away somewhere, or this endless rain was keeping him at home. Now that I look back on it, I wonder if he was being coerced into something.'

'And there was nothing you could tell me about this man who might identify him? Age? Ethnicity? Eye colour?'

'He was white. I couldn't see his hair, but I think he had blue eyes. I didn't look too hard, you know? Oh, there was one thing. When he got off, he leaned on the pole by the door like people in a hurry always tend to do. And there was something about the little finger on his … ah … right hand, it would have been. It kind of stuck out at a weird angle, like it was crooked or something.'

Slim lifted a hand and pulled his little finger downwards until the tendons wouldn't allow it to go further. 'Like this?'

'Yeah, but more. Like someone had grabbed it and tried to snap it right off.'

20

A MAN WITH A CROOKED, potentially broken finger. Slim had heard tales of Asian gangs where a finger or part of one might be removed as a penance for breaking some gang rule. Could this have been a poor man's version, or something else? An accident, a birth deformity, even a double-jointed digit?

It wasn't much to go on, but it was something, a starting point. Slim returned to Bob's street—where he noticed the house was still cordoned off by police tape—and found himself knocking on Cheryl Callow's door.

'Back again?' she said, pushing both a dog and a small child behind her as though either one might make a sudden break for the dangers of the street. 'You haven't found him yet?'

Slim shook his head. 'Not yet, I'm afraid.' He tried a reassuring smile. 'But I'm persistent. You have to be, in my line of work.'

'I suppose the BBC expect nothing less,' Cheryl said, reminding Slim whose persona he had adopted for her.

'Quite, quite. Ah, I see there's been some activity over

at Bob's place. I don't know if you could tell me what that was about?'

'Well, I don't like to gossip, but I think they might have found him dead in there. Glenda up the street said she saw a body bag being hauled out of there early one morning. Trying to sneak it out before anyone was up, so it was on the quiet. Now, why would they do that unless he'd been knocked off or something?'

'I'm not familiar with the way the police work,' Slim said. 'Something I did hear was that he was seen with a young man prior to his death. A young man who wore a hoodie and had a crooked little finger on his right hand. Does that sound familiar?'

For a moment, Cheryl's demeanour changed, the brash, know-it-all façade slipping to reveal someone else beneath, someone nervous, fearful.

'I could ask around,' she said, peering up the street, avoiding Slim's eyes. 'There might be someone who knows.'

'Do you have a lot of social issues round here?' Slim asked, aware from the general way the street looked and the groups of kids shuffling about on corners that there was only one right answer. 'Any gang trouble?'

Cheryl shook her head far too quickly. 'No, nothing like that. A few of the local kids are a bit wayward, but they're mostly harmless.'

'Right, well, if you do hear anything, you know how to contact me.'

'I have your number, that's right.'

'Thank you.'

She shut the door hard enough for Slim to consider it a slam.

He stood still for a moment, peering up into the grey sky. Was it possible Bob had got into trouble with a local gang? It seemed ridiculous, but street punks could be a sensitive lot, taking exaggerated offence at a wrong word or sideways look. Slim walked up the street, turned a corner and found himself outside a local newsagent.

The owner, a gnarled middle-aged woman who could have been younger than Slim but looked twenty years older, was only too happy to chew his ear off about the local delinquents, condemning them for shoplifting, graffiti, vandalism.

'This country's gone to the dogs,' she snapped, lighting a cigarette behind the counter, standing directly under a No Smoking sign she had likely hung herself. 'Used to be these kids would be in trade school, learning something to make themselves useful. Now they're outside at all hours, drinking, smoking, taking drugs, making trouble of themselves. I pay my taxes, and instead of spending the money filling in those bloody potholes, the council's out cleaning off spray paint, replacing the glass in the bus shelters....'

Slim listened until she paused long enough for him to politely make his excuses and leave. He walked up the street, wandering around for a while, looking for the eye of the storm. He found it in a small park, crowding around a wall behind a set of swings. A freshly empty can of Special Brew was crumpled and hit the ground as he approached. A girl in an undersized tracksuit muttered something about going to score, while two boys argued over who owed a fiver to whom. Five others stood around drinking, smoking, looking bored.

Slim walked over, hands in his pockets. The group immediately parted, spreading out, encircling him in a pincer movement, a classic battle formation. If they came at him, they would come from all sides at once. Slim eyed the nearby swings, wondering how he could use the metal frame as a barricade if necessary, increase his odds.

'I'm looking for someone,' he said. 'Any of you know a kid with a twisted little finger?' He held up his right hand. 'This one.'

A few told him to go away in no uncertain terms.

'Are you a pig?' the girl asked. 'We don't want nothing to do with pigs.'

'I can smell bacon,' another said.

Slim smiled. 'It's an honourable profession. Good salary and benefits package, and no day is ever the same. You all look about the right age to apply.'

'I knew he was a pig. We ain't done nothing.'

A couple had backed away towards the park gates, but the others that remained ghosted toughness, wanting to fight, preferring to leave.

'I just want some information. I'm looking for someone who's gone missing. A man who lives near here, or did.'

A boy from the background stepped forward. He had a guarded look about him, a way of standing with his head dipped to one side as though to better ride a punch. A scar ran down one side of his eye, and a fresh bruise turned it crimson.

'Harker,' he said. 'You're talking about … the Punch and Judy man. You the same man who was asking about?'

'That's me,' Slim said, as a couple of others warned the battered kid off engaging. He ignored them and took another tentative step forward; Slim sensed his look came from beyond this group, likely from the threatening corridors of his family home. He clenched a fist, wanting to punch something that wasn't here.

'Don't know no crooked finger guy but I heard summink.'

'Shut up, C—'

'I—'

'C, he's a pig.'

The kid the others called "C" looked about to say something but the group mentality had closed around him. Ducking his head, he shuffled back into the group.

Slim pulled a card from his pocket, wishing he had more. He set it down on the ground then put a stone over it.

'My number,' he said. 'I'm a private investigator. I also have a list of convictions as long as my arm, so let's just say I have an uneasy relationship with the police. I don't need your names, just what, if anything, you know.' He smiled as he sat back on his haunches, still surprised no kick had come in. 'Think of it as giving back to the community.'

The expletives came thick and fast as he stood up, but no one jumped him, no one attempted to wrap a steel pole or a lump of concrete around his neck. He turned around and smiled. At least a couple of them looked like they wanted a way out, a chance to do something more productive than stand around in a nondescript park drinking Special Brew in the middle of the morning.

'I could do with some help,' he said as he started to walk away. People to knock on doors, ask questions. The card's there on the floor. Or if you can remember a name, it's John Hardy. Look me up. There'll be a phone or an email address online … somewhere.'

He walked away, not looking back. The defiance came as he reached the park's gate: a thrown can, full, but it landed too far to his right to have been properly aimed; the thrower was setting a mark, making a point. Slim watched beer fizzing out of a puncture hole in the side, remembering days when he would have scrambled in the dirt to save that beer, licked the grass and stones if necessary.

Hopefully those days were gone. But one never knew.

He walked out of the park, not looking back.

21

'HE WAS MEDICALLY DISCHARGED,' Don said. 'I had a dig around an old records site and then found the names of a couple of his former squad lieutenants. I've emailed you the details, but one was still active during my own time in the Armed Forces. I gave him a call.'

'And?'

'Private Robert Harker was a member of 3 Commando Brigade set ashore at San Carlos beach as part of Operation Sutton on 21st May, 1982. During the subsequent Battle of Goose Green he received a shrapnel wound in his lower leg. During the fighting he was separated from his squadron. Here's where things get a little uncertain. My contact said Bob just kind of vanished. He was considered MIA for a while, then later showed up in a hospital in Rio Gallegos on the Argentine mainland. It appeared he had been airlifted out by retreating Argentinian forces, although how he had ended up with them was something of a mystery.'

'He was a prisoner of war?'

'My contact said that while Bob had been kept under

military guard, after the ceasefire he was officially released. However, due to the sensitivity of the political situation, plus the status of his own injury, he wasn't returned to the UK until the October of 1982, nearly four months after the war ended.'

'Was he ever made a public figure because of it?'

'My contact said that after his discharge, Bob effectively disappeared. He returned to his home town and would no longer entertain contact from his former squad mates. My contact hadn't seen or heard from him in over forty years.'

'Thanks, Don.'

Slim hung up. He had further questions, but right now his brain was full. Bob Harker, like himself, had been a military man, and like himself, had likely seen things in combat he wished to forget. It was no surprise to Slim that Bob had left the Armed Forces behind; there was a good reason why few former servicemen would ever talk about their experiences, and why the rates of suicide and mental illness were so high. Bob had withdrawn to a world where he felt safe, where he could begin the gradual process of trying to forget.

Slim went back down to the pier to clear out his head with a little sea air. As May began to drag the year towards summer, he was able to leave his coat unzipped for the first time, and when the sun broke through the clouds it was almost warm. He stood on the sand where Reggie claimed to have seen Bob's body and looked up and down the beach, wondering in which direction, if someone had moved it, as Reggie claimed, it might have gone.

The beach up here was steep, mounds of piled sand left to dry and turn into dunes away from the high-water mark. To either side was an arduous slog to the nearest steps. From there, of course, it was another steep climb up to the promenade with its wide street and facing line of houses and hotels, stalls and excursion cabins. No body, had there been one, could have been taken that way without being seen, which left only one option.

Out to sea.

He had just one contact who knew anything about boats, so he made a call to the son-in-law of the photographer he had met at random after meeting with Fiona, and asked for a private tour around the bay.

At the northern end of the main beach was a stone causeway reaching out into the water that created a small harbour for leisure boats. A couple of sailing clubhouses stood overlooking the water and a launching ramp. William Hunter was a towering, broad-shouldered man, a little younger than Slim, who shook Slim's hand with a grip that felt used to hauling ropes and wrestling monster fish out of the sea. He waved Slim down a set of stone steps to where a narrow blue dinghy waited, outboard motor idling in the water. Slim climbed in, William started the engine, and they powered out into the bay.

'My father-in-law mentioned you,' William said as they arced around to view the Grand Pier from the seaward side. 'I wondered if you'd call. Are you some sort of researcher?'

'Something like that,' Slim said. 'I'm researching for … a book. How safe would you say the beach is for swimming?'

It was a casual question, one that could easily be answered by one of the many signboards along the promenade, but it got William talking, unleashing a volley of local knowledge that was exactly what Slim was looking for.

'You're not going to have any trouble if you follow the rules,' he said. 'But you should stay away from the low water line. The mud can be thick enough to trap you, and the tidal range can be as much as fifteen metres. The water can move at ten miles an hour so you can be underwater in minutes if you're not careful.'

'Does the water come right up to the promenade?'

'It can, in spring tides. I've seen it come right over the sea wall. Most of the time however, you'll have a hundred metres or so of shore even at high tide.'

'I read somewhere that the Bristol Channel has the second highest tidal range in the world.'

William smiled proudly. 'After the Bay of Fundy in Nova Scotia. You're right. It's due to facing right out into the Atlantic, coupled with the way the channel narrows. It can make for some great deep water fishing out in the middle there, and some great sand for the beaches. You don't want to mess around though. The sea can be a dangerous beast.'

'Not good to fall off a boat then?'

'Nope. The current can be treacherous. Depending which way it's going, you'll either be dumped into the mud of the Severn Estuary or sucked right out to sea.'

'Never to be seen again?' Slim said it with a smile on his face, and William laughed.

'That's right.'

They floated in silence for a while, looking at the distant Grand Pier extending out into the sea. Behind them to the north was the old pier, while further to the south was a jutting headland.

'It's dramatic,' Slim said at last. 'I've never been much of one for the water.' He gave a grim smile, remembering. 'I've had a couple of bad experiences.'

'That can put you off, I imagine. You're perfectly safe though, if you're careful with the conditions.'

'How hard is it to launch a boat off the beach?'

'It depends on the conditions, really. High tide is easier for larger boats, as a trailer could get stuck in the mud at low tide. For anything small enough to be dragged, you could get out at any time.'

William took them in close to the Grand Pier, until they could see into the shadows beneath the huge metal frame supporting the structure. You could walk beneath it at low tide, or at high tide, you could have sailed a small boat between its struts.

'Is it safe to sail underneath?' Slim asked.

'If your boat is small enough. You risk hitting something, though.'

'If I wanted to sail a boat out from the beach without being noticed, how would I do it?'

William laughed. 'At night,' he said. 'Even then someone would see if you had any light at all.'

'Daytime?'

'The only way would be in thick fog. It can be terrible here, especially in the spring and autumn when the temperature changes quickly. You wouldn't be able to see where you were going, though.'

They headed further out into the channel and headed north, until they were moving past the old pier and the rocky island it connected to the mainland.

'Chalk and cheese,' William said. 'My father-in-law is obsessed with this old thing. He thinks the other one is straight up tacky. He's got a point, but that's the kind of thing people like about these seaside towns, isn't it?'

Slim nodded. 'From a certain perspective it could be called charming,' he said. 'It depends on how you look at it. I have to say I'm with your father-in-law. Less people around.'

'I'd take you in, but it's private property now and we'd

be in trouble if we were spotted. I've been on it before, though. It's quite the curio.'

Slim looked at his watch. It had taken roughly seven minutes to get from the Grand Pier to the North Pier by boat. Had Bob had transport, he could easily have made it back to his supposed final resting place after being seen going on to the old pier. The question that remained was why had he done it in the first place?

William, citing another planned trip, headed back to the harbour. Slim thanked him, and took a business card, in case he had further questions. Back at his B&B, it didn't take long to find out that on the day Reggie had found Bob's body, high tide had been just an hour earlier than the time the call had been logged to police. The weather conditions had been overcast, with fog around. It seemed possible to Slim that in the time Reggie was occupied by calling the police, Bob's body could have been dragged down the beach and taken out by boat beneath the pier, with the fog providing additional cover.

How could he ever prove it, though? And how would he ever know who was responsible?

22

ROBERT TILLER SMILED as the kids assembled in the town library ahhed at the vicious scar running across his side, from just below his armpit to his stomach.

'And if I haven't already put you off ever joining a gang, let this teach you. One centimetre left and I was dead. I'm obviously not, but I feel it pull every time I turn my head or twist my body. It's a constant reminder. I got this over a bag of forged passports. That's all. I asked for two hundred quid over the agreed price, thinking the other guy was desperate.' He patted the scar. 'Turned out that he was.'

The children clapped as Robert lowered his shirt and signed off with a bit of information on support groups and helplines. As the children dispersed, Slim waited until the library staff had finished their thanks and moved off, then approached Robert as he was packing photographs and books into a bag.

'Excuse me.'

Robert looked up and smiled. Sixty-two, Slim knew from a search online, his face was weathered and jagged like ancient moorland rocks, and his eyes still held a little of the old hardness. You could change your clothes, Slim knew, but often you couldn't change yourself. Robert walked the line of anti-gang advocacy, but that hard, merciless gang enforcer would always be hiding in there, ready if needed.

'I saw you back there,' Robert said. 'How did you enjoy the talk?'

'It was informative. My name's John Hardy, but people call me Slim. I sent you an email.'

'Ah, yes. My wife acts as my secretary, and she mentioned it.'

'If you had time for a coffee—'

'You look like a man of the world, John,' Robert said, continuing to pack his bag. 'As you get older, you tend to pick and choose what you remember. I've done my time, and now I'm giving back, but I'm not interested in an interrogation.'

'That's not what I'm after. As I said in my email, I'm interested in knowing about your association with Jackie Ackerman, a member of your old gang—'

'—murdered by Frederick Bowles in 1995. I know. I got your email.'

'I'd just like to know—'

'I'm sorry,' Robert said. He put up a hand, almost to push Slim away. He winced, not meeting Slim's eyes as he added, 'The problem is, that while I've left that life behind, not everyone has. Not all of those people are incarcerated or dead. There are still people out there I'm not prepared to talk about.'

'It could be related to a murder.'

'Then I wish the police good luck.' He shouldered his bag. 'I'm sorry, but I have another appointment. I hope you found the talk useful.' He clapped a hand on Slim's shoulder as he passed. 'Stay away from gangs, John.' The words sounded more like a threat than a warning. Slim turned and watched Robert leave, the other man not looking back.

$\sim$

SLIM IDLED FOR A WHILE, looking through a few local history books at pictures of the two piers, that of the new more often than not in vibrant colours, the old in sepia or black and white. The weather had taken a turn for the worse, so he hunkered under his coat as he waited for a bus on the street outside. Just as it pulled in a clear fifteen minutes late, his phone rang.

The caller had rung off before he had taken a seat near the rear, but the only other passengers were both young girls wearing modern headphones. Slim pulled out his phone, checked the number, then called back.

'Hello?' came a quiet mutter at the other end of the unknown number.

'You called me?' Slim asked.

'Yeah, I … met you in the park the other day.'

The quiet boy, the one the others called C, Slim remembered.

The boy said he had some information. They arranged a place to meet. Slim walked down the bus to ask the driver about routes, then got off, changing buses to head across town.

He met C outside an Asian takeaway and offered to buy him a hamburger. The boy had a fresh black eye on the left side, the skin a dark crimson, swollen and sore. He winced as he sat down, suggesting there were other bruises, out of sight.

'Who did that?' Slim asked.

The boy shrugged. 'It doesn't matter.'

'It does.'

Another shrug. 'I went back, found your card where they'd kicked it. One of the girls saw, must have made a call. Couple of guys jumped me on the way home.'

Slim seethed, clenching his fists under the table. He stared at the wall until his heart had slowed enough for him to talk without inflection.

'I'm sorry that happened to you,' he said. 'I didn't want anyone to get hurt.'

'Would have happened sooner or later.'

Slim allowed himself to look at the boy, at the light brown of faded bruises, the guarded look, the fine, almost indistinct lines of previously broken skin. A whipping post, kicked across paths, not left alone long enough to find his own. He was uncomfortably tall and thin, easily six-three though with a worrying lack of muscles, still a braggable scalp for a school bully.

'They call you C. Is that your name?'

'Chris.'

Slim nodded. A name out of fashion for people of his age; the boy sounded awkward just saying it.

'Those clowns often go after you?'

Chris shrugged. 'Not much going on around here. Usually off their heads too. Better than home.'

'Having your face blackened by a group of losers is better than home?'

Chris nodded. 'At least I can walk away.'

'How old are you?'

'Sixteen. Last month.'

'Jesus.'

'I get it. I'm tall for my age.'

'You're in school?'

Chris shrugged. Slim made a mental note of the time of year.

'You're on study leave?'

'Suppose.'

Chris was shifting on his seat, looking ready to leave. Slim pushed uncomfortable feelings aside and tried to concentrate on why they were there.

'You said you had information.'

'Yeah, suppose. Not much. I just seen him, like.'

'Who? The guy with the bad finger? Or Bob Harker?'

'Both. Together.'

Slim leaned back, letting his questions settle. Too fast and the answers would come fast also. Maybe something would be missed.

'You live near Bob?'

'Round the corner. When I'm there.'

'Can you tell me in your own words what you saw?'

'The guy was dealing him something. I'd see him up the road by the newsagent there, waiting for his deals. I was just hanging out down the park, like.'

'Late at night?'

'Dunno. Ten, eleven, maybe.'

'You're out that late?'

'I live with me granddad. He gambles. Gets upset if he loses. It's better to wait 'til he's home and asleep.'

'I get it. So you were outside. You saw Bob buying something off this guy? How do you know who they were?'

'The Punch and Judy man—Bob—he's got this limp, see. Kind of leans in to the left when he walks. Plus, he's got weird clown hair. I seen him in a coat without a cap. Damn near filled the hood.'

Slim had seen pictures, and the limp fitted with the shrapnel wound he'd received in the Falklands. 'And the other guy?'

'Didn't see him well. Looks like how a dealer always looks, you know. Hoodie, jeans, walks all shifty, head bowed. Don't blame him. There are cameras everywhere.'

'Why are you telling me this? Why was talking to me worth getting beaten up for?'

Chris's bottom lip trembled. He looked about to cry.

'I saw him once,' he said. 'Before Mum died and Dad went down. Saw him on the beach there. Ruffled my hair after the show. Last time I can remember life not being a disaster.'

Chris stuck a chip in his mouth, then abruptly started eating the hamburger in a rush. Slim waited until it was gone. Chris gave a contented sigh then went back to staring at the table.

'You have a part-time job?'

Chris shook his head. 'Like, no way. The pay sucks round here and there ain't nothing anyway, except like working in the supermarket, and then you'll always see someone you know.'

'I'm trying to find out what happened to Bob Harker,' Slim said. 'He's been missing more than a month and the only lead I have is from a shaky source, to say the least. There's other stuff I'm not sure I can talk about, but right now I'm getting nowhere. I need someone to do some donkey work for me. It might not be interesting, but I can pay. You're young; you're tall; I know you can walk the streets. Can you use a computer?'

'I had an Xbox until Granddad sold it—'

Slim grimaced. 'The internet? You can use it at the library.'

'Yeah, 'course.'

'Good. Are you interested? Might only be for a few weeks—'

The light that appeared in Chris's face brought a tear

to Slim's eye. It had been a long time since he'd reached out to someone, offered a helping hand. He was a lone wolf, but once in a while even he needed company. The last person he'd helped had sent him an email a couple of months ago to say she'd been accepted onto a forensics degree course. Sometimes people could be saved.

'Yeah, just let me know what you need me to do.'

'First of all, I need to know Bob Harker. I have a couple of pictures, that's all. I need you to go online, use them to search for more images, then find out who took them, when they took them, why they took them. Contact as many people as you can. The smallest detail could be critical. Then we go door to door. I want names of every person who can recall seeing Bob from January to April of this year.'

Chris grinned, hands on the table edge, a boxer ready to climb back off the canvas.

'I'm on it,' he said.

23

A PHONE CALL to the local harbour authority proved fruit-less. Only boats over a certain size were required to register their presence. Anything small or portable could come and go as they wished.

Following the assumption that Reggie Bowles was telling the truth—mostly because he had little option—Slim turned his attention to who might have had a reason to murder Bob. Who were his enemies? And in the absence of those, who were his competitors?

The line of thought led him back to the theatre inside the Grand Pier. With a break in the relentlessly poor weather allowing the streets to dry out, he headed there on foot, taking a circuitous route, trying to get a feel for the town and its streets, the good areas and bad, feeling how it breathed, imploring it to reveal its secrets.

If only stone could talk. Something had seen what happened to Bob Harker, and something knew why.

He found the theatre in the middle of a rehearsal for an upcoming performance. Marius was busy, sitting in front of the small stage beside an animated older woman who seemed to defy the chair below her, on her feet constantly as she directed the stage actors, calling a halt every few lines to order someone a step forward, two steps back. Fiona stood at the top of the stairs, leaning against the wall with her arms folded. As Slim approached through the open door, the creak of the step gave him away, and she turned.

'Sorry … the door was open. Is this a bad time?'

Fiona shook her head. 'They're just getting started. This is the part most people don't see.'

'They're not wearing costumes. It's hard to tell who's who.'

'We're not up to dress rehearsals yet.'

Slim turned, nodding at a new poster pinned up behind the reception desk. 'Is that it? The Forgotten Sailor?'

Fiona smiled. 'How did you guess?'

'Directed by Amanda Smart. Is that her?'

'Yes, the famous Amanda Smart. The lead is Keith Anderson. That's the man there in the centre. He's an old thespian.' Fiona smiled. 'He played a tree in Hamlet about thirty years ago.'

'You sound bitter.'

'He's local. He took me out for a drink once, forgot to mention he was married.'

'Ouch. Old wounds.'

'The old Casanova is yet to recognise me and this is the third day of stage rehearsals.'

Slim smiled. 'You must have changed your hair.'

Fiona grinned and flicked the bottom of her mani-cured bob. 'You're probably right.'

'Either that or his eyes have gone.'

'Well, he is significantly older than me.'

'That's what I meant.'

Their conversation was abruptly muted as the director yelled 'Stop!' far louder than was necessary, then climbed out of her seat and proceeded to berate the actors from below the stage.

'This Ms Smart ... she's fearsome,' Slim said. 'I'm surprised they put up with her.'

'She has pedigree,' Fiona said. 'And something else ... you can keep a secret?'

'My whole life is a secret,' Slim said.

'They're filming the production for television. One of those live shows. It'll run on one of the big streaming services around Christmas. It's the kind of thing that could make a career, so they'll put up with a lot more than the amateur lots will.'

'Really? Good luck to them.'

Amanda Smart shouted 'Action!' and the scene continued. Slim muttered something about coming back later and was just turning away when the lead character exclaimed, 'And I find myself at the funfair gates! Oh, oracle, what is it you see?'

A man shuffled on from the side of the stage, two stagehands holding up a plywood theatre in front of him. One hand rose, a skeletal puppet leaning over the wooden edge.

'Dear marooned sailor,' came a reedy voice. 'I fear there is no hope for one such as thee.'

'Got that right,' Fiona muttered.

'Is that what I think it is?' Slim asked. 'A Punch and Judy show?'

'From hell,' Fiona said. 'He's been washed up on some kind of purgatory island. The puppets give him advice on how to reform his character and lead a better life. Once he's found his morals he can leave.'

Slim, intrigued, watched for a few minutes more as the

puppet instructed the marooned sailor in some morally just task, the sailor lamenting the whole way.

'It's very Greek tragedy,' Fiona said. 'Personally, I think it's going to be a huge flop.'

'Is it an old story? I'm afraid I'm not one for the theatre.'

'No, one of the actors wrote it, apparently.' Fiona nodded at a handful of players standing around the edge of the stage. 'That woman there, wearing the hat. She plays the sailor's estranged daughter.'

'She wrote it?'

'Amanda Smart has an open submission page on her website. If she picks up your script, you could find yourself with a career.'

Slim was about to ask the girl's name when his phone began to buzz in his pocket. He muttered an apology to Fiona then quickly headed outside.

Karen Tasker had left three missed calls. Slim called her back.

'Karen?'

'Slim. Sorry not to be in touch. There's been something of a development. We think we might have found him.'

24

'THERE.' Karen pointed at the screen. 'Getting off the bus. That's him.'

Slim failed to share her enthusiasm. The picture was grainy, black and white, evening shadows stretching across the forecourt of Bristol Bus Station, making it impossible to see the people in detail. Had it been anyone else there wouldn't have been much call for doubt, but as the figure stooped, pulling a rucksack out of the bus's undercarriage, before shouldering it and limping away, Slim had to admit that the details were there. The hat, the bag, the limp.

Bob Harker.

'When was this?' Slim asked.

'22nd of April. Approximately ten days after Reggie reported finding Bob's body.'

'So it looks like he came back from the dead.'

'Or was never dead in the first place. Or was never even there. Reggie is known to the police. We should have been more sceptical.'

'Do you have more footage?'

'Working on getting tape from everywhere within a hundred-metre radius. See if we can pick up a trail.'

'It's three weeks cold.'

'But it's something. What do you have?' Her tone was uncharacteristically harsh, and as Slim looked at her, she apologised. 'I'm sorry. This case is driving me to despair. You'd think there'd be a trail as wide as the beach at low bloody tide, but nothing we've found so far tells us anything.'

'How many do you have working the case?'

Karen sighed. 'Myself and two junior officers.' She shrugged. 'And you.'

'The budget's that bad, is it?'

'We're still waiting on the final coroner's report, but murder has been ruled out. It's corpse abandonment plus a missing persons. And with no disrespect to Bob, no one's looking for him. If he were a child, or a spouse, had a family hassling us for answers....' She trailed off, shaking her head. 'Did you hear about that woman whose death went unnoticed for four years? Had it not been for you sticking your nose in—'

'I have a habit of that.'

She smiled. 'Yeah. I noticed.'

'If you have tapes that need to be viewed, let me have them.'

'You have time?'

'I hired an assistant.'

'Expanding?'

He shrugged. 'Something like that. My eyes aren't what they used to be.'

'I'll get you what I can. I'm not sure where we go from here. It's all I can do to keep the case open. Abandonment, particularly with no signs of abuse or neglect, is a relatively minor crime. We're still yet to identify the woman. If we could pin Harker on a kidnapping charge, that would certainly ramp things up a bit.'

'Kidnapping?'

Karen sighed again. 'I'm clutching at straws. There's no evidence that Bob did anything other than care for her to the best of his ability. Albeit in total secrecy.'

Karen had to go back to work, but she left Slim a copy of the video along with the other details that she had. A passenger list for the bus Bob had supposedly arrived on, although nine passengers had paid in cash at the counter, leaving no personal details. He had fourteen other names, plus the driver, however, meaning some more work for Chris. He smiled. The boy was enthusiastic, even if he was yet to find anything of note.

The local bus station where Bob had caught the bus had let them down, with the camera covering the ticket machines and counter being out of order. However, Bob was distinctive enough that someone might remember seeing him.

Karen had printed missing posters and placed them at the local bus and train stations as well as at those in Bristol. She had told Slim she would need more detail if she were to get the budget to expand the search further afield.

∾

'IT'S NOT MUCH, but this is what I have so far,' Chris said, opening an old laptop Slim had lent him and turning it around to show Slim the screen. 'Got these off social media.' He grinned, revealing a broken left canine. 'Old people tend to forget to make their accounts private, while kids will accept any old friend request.'

'Anything we can work with?'

Chris flicked through a handful of family pictures,

mostly showing groups standing alongside a smiling Bob Harker. He seemed very much a man of the people, thumbs up, even lending a kid his hat for one windswept shot, his hair in the process of taking off. And there was a short video of a family in the middle of setting up their towels and windbreaks while in the background Bob could be seen, shuffling about, setting up his portable theatre while a handful of kids looked on. Slim watched the video through a couple of times, then looked at Chris and nodded.

'You've done well.'

Chris beamed. 'I can find more. I'm sure of it. Did you find what you were looking for?'

Slim gave a slow nod. Some evidence to back up that Bob was a popular seaside entertainer. That he looked how Slim thought, that he looked like the person in the CCTV footage from Bristol Bus Station.

'Keep looking,' he said. 'See how far back you can find footage. I want to know if there are any changes in his attitude, his demeanour.'

Even as Chris nodded, Slim wondered at the words coming out of his own mouth. He barely recognised them. They came from a man clutching at air, out of ideas. As Chris began to put the laptop away, Slim cleared his throat.

'When you look at those, what do you see?'

Chris gave an awkward shrug. 'I dunno really. It's a beach scene, isn't it?'

'That's all I see too.'

'I mean, it's a bit old fashioned, isn't it? Like something out of the sixties. That old Punch and Judy guy, I mean, you don't see them now, do you?'

'No, you don't.' Slim forced a smile. 'Thanks again for your efforts. Keep trying.'

'What is it this guy has done?' Chris asked abruptly, then immediately gave a pensive twitch as though he'd spoken out of line.

'I'm not sure,' Slim said. He had given Chris little detail about the case but the boy perhaps deserved a little more rope. 'It's possible he is connected to a crime, or maybe the victim of one. I was initially interested in this case because I was approached by a man who claimed to have found his body, only for it to disappear.'

Chris nodded. 'Oh. Where did it go?'

'I have no idea. It was seen on the sand under the pier. By the time the police had reached the spot, it had gone. However, the man who reported it has a record of wasting police time.'

'He just wants attention,' Chris said, looking at the tabletop.

'I'm sorry?'

'That's what it is, these days, isn't it? Everyone wants to be noticed for something, and if they don't have anything worthwhile or any special skill, they do something dumb online or they commit some crime.'

Slim smiled. 'What do you want to be noticed for?'

'I don't want to be noticed. It's rare.' Chris sighed. 'Not being noticed hurts less.'

25

SLIM STARED at the grainy image of Bob walking away from the bus, his pack looming on his shoulders. He had tasked Chris with tracking down the people he could name on the passenger list. Karen had failed to obtain an official warrant so Chris had to trawl through social media in search of them, but to Slim's surprise the boy had taken to it with gusto, promising to find something of value to the investigation.

Slim, feeling like he was dropping the ball a little, sent another email to Robert Tiller, asking about his knowledge of the E-boys and Jackie Ackerman, this time with a more aggressive tone, suggesting that if Tiller really wanted to help keep young people away from gangs, he should be more open with his information. It was a deliberate attempt to provoke a response, but sometimes the only way to get at the honey was to kick the bees' nest, then take cover until the fallout was over. Concerned Tiller might still have gangland connections, Slim changed B&Bs, moving to a different residence a couple of streets away.

Karen's call came after several days of silence. 'Slim,

the full autopsy report on the woman in Bob's house is in,' she said. 'I can send you a copy.'

'Thank you. What was the official cause of death?'

'Terminal cancer. Bowel, but it had metastasised to her liver and lungs. Now, here's the thing. No traces of cancer-related drugs were found in her body. However, there were traces of tetrahydrocannabinol found in her urine and hair. Also known as THC, it's the active component of marijuana. Based on the levels found, it looks like she was using it for pain relief.'

The man with the crooked finger. 'Bob was buying it for her?'

'It's possible. It's available legally from a doctor in certain cases but the patient would have to be registered. 'We've found no identification details for her at all. However, the circumstances suggest that Bob was caring for her at his home to the best of his ability.'

'Was there any likelihood of euthanasia? As it's still considered murder in this country.'

'Nothing in the findings. But decomposition had set in, and some data would have been lost.'

'That's unfortunate.'

Karen sighed. 'It means the case will likely be down-graded again. Less budget, less chance of finding Harker.'

'I've been looking at that video,' Slim said. 'I'm trying to find eyewitnesses. If that's really him, we need more footage.'

'We're still collecting information.'

Slim smiled. 'Which is police-speak for you don't have anything yet.'

Karen laughed. 'Bingo. But we're working on it.'

They hung up, and Slim opened the email containing the autopsy report on his laptop. The woman was esti-mated to be between eighty and ninety years old, white, approximately 170cm tall. Weight at death: 44 kilogrammes. Cause of death: organ failure due to terminal cancer.

The coroner had noted that the state of decomposition suggested she had been dead for roughly six weeks, two weeks longer than Bob had been missing. What had happened during that two-week period? Sightings of Bob might help, but it would take forever to canvass the neighbourhood. He could set Chris on the case but it wouldn't be enough. Bob's death just wasn't important enough for the police to employ the manpower required for such an effort.

He had to make it so.

An hour later he called Chris and arranged to meet his new assistant at a nearby fast-food restaurant. Slim chewed down a hamburger without much enthusiasm, but he had timed his mid-afternoon meal perfectly for the coffee to be left over from lunch.

'I need to kick a hornets' nest,' he told Chris. 'This case is threatening to go cold. You see, Bob's not the only person involved. A woman's decomposing corpse was found in an upstairs bedroom at his home.'

He explained to Chris what he knew so far about the woman's body found in Bob's bedroom. Chris listened with wide eyes then simply muttered 'No way!' at the end.

'At the moment we have a man potentially on the run for abandoning a body. If the death was natural causes, which is what it appears to be, at worst he's looking at a year in prison. More likely he'd get a suspended sentence. She was an old woman; he's an old man. No family looking for either. Not enough people care to figure this thing out.'

'What do you think happened?' Chris said, looking at

Slim the way a child might look at a parent, expecting nothing less than oracle powers of knowledge.

Slim frowned. He was often at the mercy of his own thoughts, and had often asked the question of countless others, aware that sometimes the root of an answer could come from speculation as well as from hard facts. Rarely, however, had the question been asked of him so directly.

He sipped coffee that had gone cold, collecting his thoughts.

'I think … this woman meant a lot to Bob Harker, but for reasons I'm yet to understand, he kept her presence secret. Perhaps she had fallen foul of the law, maybe unjustly. Maybe she had enemies, and Bob was doing her a favour. None of the evidence from his property says she was imprisoned against her will or mistreated in any way. It looks like he did everything possible to make her final years as comfortable as he could.'

Chris gave a thoughtful nod. 'Not a criminal. An illegal. Someone off the boats, maybe. Have the police run her DNA?'

'Against the missing persons database—'

'Have they tried any of those websites that trace family?'

'I can ask.'

'Or get a sample and we could do it.'

Slim smiled. 'You think like me.'

26

POLICE TAPE still surrounded Bob Harker's place, but there were no police guarding it that Slim could see, no unmarked car, no figure hiding behind a drape in a window across the street. Chris spotted the alarm wired across the back door, but Slim had come prepared, attaching a little device he had borrowed from but failed to return to an old Armed Forces acquaintance, a device which overrode the trip switch, allowing him to use his lock-pick to get inside.

Then, using a torch covered with a cloth to dampen the beam, Slim headed upstairs in search of a DNA sample, leaving Chris to keep watch by the front door, under strict instructions not to touch anything.

The upper floor had a strong smell of disinfectant, and for a moment its association with alcohol made Slim pause. A year without a drink was his longest in some time, but he was only ever a moment away.

Focus.

He took a deep breath and opened the door into the bedroom.

It had been thoroughly cleaned and the body removed, of course. The house had been searched and perhaps some items removed, but a lot of the contents remained. Slim, wearing rubber gloves, picked up a hair caught in the frame of a wheelchair folded up behind the bedroom door, slipping it into an evidence bag. He then did the same with a well-thumbed paperback book and a small woman's slipper. A few more swabs from bed frames, door handles, and tabletops, and he felt sure he had enough.

He went downstairs, calling for Chris.

'I'm in here.'

The workroom by the front door. Slim frowned as he went inside, worried Chris might have disturbed something, but Chris was leaning over a table, staring at a half-finished puppet lying amidst a pile of shredded paper.

Slim glanced around. While some drawers had been opened in a cabinet against one wall, their contents rifled through, the workroom looked much as he remembered, the police having perhaps focused their search on the kitchen, living room and bedrooms.

'He's making it by gluing strips of paper one over the other,' Chris said. 'Kind of like papier mâché, but without pulping the paper. No idea why. Perhaps it's some old technique or something. Or maybe he's just using what material he had available.'

He reached out for the puppet.

'Don't—'

Chris snatched his hand away and shrank back as though waiting to be hit. 'Sorry, I just … I just wanted to see what it said.'

'What do you mean?'

'Those bits of paper. It looked like Spanish. I did it at school for two years. I'm supposed to have an exam next week, but well….'

'Can you read it?'

'Only a few words. I'm not much good. That word, that's beach, I think. That one is ship. I think that's money, but I'm not sure.'

Slim pulled a plastic evidence bag out of his pocket. 'Gather up what you can.' As Chris started to tentatively gather up the scrap paper, Slim pointed to the puppet. 'That too.'

'What about those others?' Chris nodded at a line of puppets on a shelf. Some were painted and complete, others still unfinished.

Tampering with a crime scene, in this case might hold a harsher sentence than the crime. He had come on a whim, neglecting to tell Karen beforehand.

'Leave them,' he said. 'If we need more, I'll speak to the police.'

But would he? As Chris gathered the last scraps into a bag, Slim wondered if he was making a mistake.

They headed out the way they had come, reactivating the alarm on the way out. It was possible the police would have no further need to come here. With their own search complete, they were perhaps waiting on whether Bob's relatives appeared to make a claim. According to Karen, no will had been found. If no family member could be traced, Bob's property would eventually be turned over to the state, a legal process that could take years, depending on his financial situation.

Slim drove Chris back to his house, parking across the street.

'That one?' Slim asked, pointing to a tatty terrace with lights on in the downstairs window.

'Yeah.' Chris nodded, but Slim saw the look of fear in his eyes.

'Are you sure?'

'I'm good.'

'You're free tomorrow? Or should you be studying for your exams?'

A small smile. 'Yeah, maybe. I'll have time.'

'I suggest you brush up on your Spanish. We might need it.'

'Sure.'

Chris got out, walking across the street. Slim watched him go inside, heart fluttering as the front door closed and a light came on in the hall. Another light appeared upstairs, then the hall light went off. For a moment, an upstairs curtain was tweaked back and Chris's face appeared. Slim nodded, then put the idling car into gear and pulled away.

27

'SLIM? Always good to hear from you.' A chuckle. 'I'm never so sure about what you might want.'

Slim smiled. Kay Skelton was an old friend from the Armed Forces who now worked in forensic linguistics. Kay's willingness to help when many of Slim's other acquaintances had turned their backs meant Slim had often made requests that went far outside Kay's area of expertise.

'Do you know anyone who speaks Spanish?'

Kay laughed. 'Compared to some of the things you've asked me, that's an easy one. You need a translation done?'

'I think so. We're not sure what it relates to, but if you could have a look.'

'We?'

Slim smiled. 'I've hired an assistant. At least for now.'

'Going up in the world?'

'Maybe.'

'If you could photograph what you have, or better, send me the original copies, that would be great.'

'Thanks, Kay.'

∽

CHRIS HAD MADE a list of websites offering DNA history so Slim signed up for all of them. Most required a saliva sample but with no way to provide one he made some phone calls and asked for alternative methods. A couple of sites refused him outright, but one site which claimed a connection, to a shared database of DNA history information, told him to provide a swab or a piece of material in a sterile solution. Slim created three samples: one from part of the hair, another from the slipper, and one from a lower corner of the paperback book.

He posted them, paying extra for an express service, with results due within two weeks.

It was something.

With little else to do but wait, he went for a walk on the beach. May was creeping towards June, the traditional start of summer, but it seemed no one had told the weather, which buffeted the handful of strollers and dog walkers with powerful gusts of wind, threatening to drag anything smaller than a poodle into the grey shore break. Spray came from both the sea and the lumpy black clouds overhead, differentiated only by the taste of salt on Slim's tongue.

Cowering beneath the struts of the Grand Pier, he tried to call Chris, but received no answer. Similarly, Karen ignored his call, but when he took out his phone a few minutes later inside the pier's sheltered entrance, he found a missed call from an unidentified number. He called back, but no one answered.

Getting coffee at a stall inside the pier, he took out his notebook and went over what he knew so far.

Bob was missing, potentially dead, potentially on the run, last seen at Bristol Bus Station on the 22nd of April, ten days after his body was reported unresponsive by Reggie Bowles, supposedly then disappearing in the thirty-minute period it took the police to arrive. A body was found in his house, belonging to an elderly and terminally ill woman, who had seemingly been treated well prior to her death in the two weeks before Bob's disappearance. And in the days before, Bob had been seen trying to get onto the abandoned pier north of the town, and also on a local bus with a young man with a crooked finger.

Slim wanted to throw the notebook across the floor. Of all the investigations he had done, he had never come so far but discovered so little.

'Hello, stranger.'

He looked up to see Fiona standing over him, holding a paper cup with a plastic lid.

'Penny for your thoughts?'

Slim sighed. 'I'd go as high as a fiver if it would make much difference. How's the theatre?'

Fiona rolled her eyes. 'The rehearsals continue to roll on. Ms. Smart shouts at people and Marius claps like it's some kind of circus. One of the stagehands quit yesterday after being bawled out for moving a section of painted background too slowly. You don't have any theatre experience, do you?'

'I'm afraid not.'

'That's too bad. You look like a man capable of lifting things.' She looked him up and down like a farmer assessing cattle at a market. 'Have you found Bob Harker yet?'

Slim shook his head, too weary to reply.

'Don't give up. Most cases go cold because people stop looking.'

'I haven't stopped looking yet.'

She sat down opposite him without being asked. 'Is there anything I can help with?'

'I doubt it. Unless you have a few hours to knock on doors.'

Fiona smiled. 'I don't think Marius would appreciate it.'

'I'm trying to establish what kind of man Bob was, in order to try to understand who might have wanted to harm him, but it seems he was a total loner outside his performances. He had no friends, no family. I've talked to a number of locals but no one seems to have known him at all.'

'Maybe he ended up that way, but perhaps he changed. Have you tried going back a few years?'

Slim frowned. 'No, I haven't.'

Fiona patted him on the arm with all the affection of a tired mother.

'Maybe give it a try.'

28

'COME ON IN, SIR.'

The excessive formality might have rankled Slim had Benjamin Redfield not been quite so smartly dressed. Easily eighty, he wore a neat shirt and tie, checked trousers and a beige tank top that failed to add any meat to a frail and skinny frame. Blue eyes beamed with intelligence but the lines and liver spots on his face showed he was entering his endgame.

'You have a lovely place,' Slim said, as Benjamin led him through into an immaculate living room.

'Thank you. I do try, although I have a young lady who comes in once a week to clean and tidy. I don't have the energy for it these days. Would you like tea?'

'If it's no trouble.'

'None at all.'

Slim took an ornate armchair while he waited for Benjamin to return a few minutes later, getting up quickly to help the old man with a tray of fine china which rattled as he walked. Benjamin briefly looked both relieved and annoyed as Slim set the tray down on a coffee table, then sat back again for Benjamin to continue.

'You said you got my name from Cheryl Callow?' Benjamin said when the teacups were safely in their hands.

'Actually, from her mother,' Slim said.

'Barbara … yes, I remember. How is she?'

'In a home, Cheryl said.'

'That's a shame. A lovely lady.' His smile dropped. 'The area used to be so nice. We moved while we could still get something for our house. I was blind to it all, but my Stephanie could see the way the area was going. All the kids running wild, those horrible druggy types moving in … twenty years we lived on that street. You wouldn't believe how much it changed. Nearly ten years since we left, and I'd dread to see it now.'

'Do you remember Robert Harker?'

Benjamin sighed, his smile dropping. 'Bob. Yes, I do.'

'Were you friends?'

'I don't think anyone was really friends with Bob. He kept himself to himself.'

Slim frowned inwardly, the answer being the one he feared.

'So you had little interaction with him?'

'Oh, I wouldn't say that. We talked from time to time. Mostly just pleasantries, sometimes more.'

'Did he have many friends?'

'I can't say that he did. Not family. He used to go away at Christmas, though. Two weeks, every year. He never said where, but it was regular as clockwork. I think he must have had family whom he stayed with.'

Slim nodded. He had put Don on the case, but so far his friend had come up with nothing.

'Then there were his lodgers,' Benjamin said. 'If you could find one of those, you might find out a little more.'

'Lodgers?'

'I know he took in students from Bristol sometimes. They would get the train in to whatever college they were studying at.'

'Were there many of these lodgers?'

'No, only one at a time.' Benjamin gave a dry chuckle that turned into a cough. 'It can't have been easy living with Bob. I think he offered overflow accommodation or something, for students who couldn't find regular housing. I used to see them come and go. They'd often only stay for a term or so, sometimes not even that long.'

'That's helpful, thanks.'

Benjamin didn't have a lot else to say, except one thing about hearing shouting on the street one night not long before he moved out.

'It wasn't uncommon by that point to have groups of yobs wandering about, but I remember that night because I thought I heard Bob's voice.'

'What did he say?'

'"I'm sorry, but I have no choice". That's it, nothing more.'

'In response to?'

'A young man berating him about timing. "Why right now?" Something like that. With a few expletives, of course. I'm afraid I closed the window on it because my dear Stephanie was already ailing at that point. I can't tell you anything else but I'm sure it was one of Bob's lodgers. A young man, I think. I really can't tell you any more than that. I never saw any others afterwards, though. I think the experience must have been too much.'

29

CHRIS STILL WASN'T ANSWERING his phone, so Slim called Donald Lane instead.

'I need to know if the universities in Bristol keep archived lists of people providing student accommodation,' he said. 'And if so, whether they have a record of who might have been using it.'

'I think you'll be lucky, but I'll try. Give me a day or so.'

'Thanks, Don. I appreciate it.'

He didn't know what difference it might make, but he had few options. The chances of uncovering Bob's fate were slipping away. He had spoken to Karen that morning, and while the police had secured several hours of CCTV footage from locations around Bristol Bus Station, none of them showed Bob. It was as though he had stepped off the bus in Bristol and subsequently vanished into thin air.

There was news from Kay, however.

'Don't have much for you yet, Slim,' Kay said. 'Got something though. Those scraps of text you sent me, they're not Spanish. They're Esperanto.'

'They're what?'

'It's an invented language. Created by L.L. Zamenhof in 1887, with the intention of being an international second language. It never took off widely but there are a couple of million people who can speak it.'

'Wait a minute … my friend said he recognised a couple of the words as Spanish. Beach and … ah … sea. That was it.'

'Hang on a sec …' Slim heard the rustle of paper, the tapping of keys. 'Yeah, he's not far off. Sea in Spanish is "mar". In Esperanto, it's "maro". Beach is "plago" with an accent on the a, as opposed to "playa" in Spanish.' Kay chuckled. 'I hope your friend won't be taking any tests.'

Slim grimaced. 'Well … so it's not Spanish? Why would someone write in Esperanto?'

'At the moment I can't tell you. What I've translated so far doesn't appear to have any specific meaning. It's like pieces of a novel. Long, extended descriptions of seascapes and coastal scenery. If this person you're looking for was using these to make puppets, it's possible they were viewed simply as an available source of scrap paper.'

'Where would a man like Bob Harker get wads of handwritten Esperanto from?'

'You're the detective, Slim. You tell me.'

HE WENT TO SEE CHRIS, partly to check up on him and partly to tell him he would need to study a little harder if he wanted to pass his Spanish exam.

A light was on in the downstairs window. Slim watched for a while from across the street, then made his way over and knocked.

After a few seconds, a shadow appeared on the other side of the frosted glass. Tall, but when the door opened, it wasn't Chris but an older man with a jutting whiskered jaw, veiny cheeks and rheumy eyes. Slim glanced down at the hand holding the door and saw scabs on the man's knuckles, a scratch up his arm.

'What do you want?'

'Where's Chris?'

'He's busy.' The man's hard eyes watched him.

'I'm a friend.'

'No, you're not. Get lost.'

Slim remembered Chris's face, the old scars, and something snapped. He stepped forward, pushing the old man aside. He had twenty years on him, perhaps, but the old man had six inches, probably a couple of stone. As Slim pushed the old man back against the wall and shouted Chris's name, he felt a hand scrabbling to get hold of him. Fingers closed over the back of his collar and jerked his head back. He caught a glimpse of Chris standing at the top of the stairs, then the old man's forehead was crashing down, striking him in the middle of the face. He staggered back, trying to catch blood in his hands, as behind him, the old man said:

'I told you to get lost.'

30

'HE'S ACCUSING ME OF ASSAULT?' Slim said, unable to keep the surprise out of his voice. He touched the padding over his reset nose. 'He's beating up his grandson, and he just rearranged my face.'

'Assault and aggravated trespass,' Karen said, giving Slim a sympathetic pat on the knee as he sat up on the edge of the hospital bed. 'You allegedly attacked him first, then forced entry into his property. Legally he acted in self-defence. You're supposed to be helping me, Slim, not acting like a vigilante for social justice.'

'He's beating up his grandson,' Slim said again.

'Social services have been alerted to problems in the home,' Karen said.

'Oh, what a relief,' Slim said, rolling his eyes. 'With their track record you could be digging the boy's grave next week.'

'You can't just take the law into your own hands.'

'Says you, providing me with information on Bob Harker.'

A small smile. 'Not all of the time.'

'Will Roger Butler drop the charges?'

'He might. He's a gambler by all accounts. Offer him some money.'

'I don't have any.'

'A famous detective like you?'

Slim almost laughed but a bolt of pain lanced across his face.

'You flatter me.'

'Get some rest.'

She pushed him gently in the chest as though to ease him back on the bed.

'Karen,' he said quietly. 'Watch out for him, if you can. Chris Butler. He's a good kid. He deserves better than that.'

She nodded. 'I'll go round with a couple of uniforms, shake the old man up a bit.' She held Slim's gaze for a moment. 'The legal way.'

'Thanks.'

Karen stood up. 'Get some rest. We still haven't found Bob Harker.'

'I know.'

'The footage we got … there's nothing. Due to drug problems, there are cameras all over that part of Bristol. He shouldn't have been able to vanish like that.'

'But he did.'

'It seems like it.'

~

THE HOSPITAL only kept him in for a day, once his nose had been reset and an MRI scan showed no signs of concussion nor further brain injury. As he walked down the street, a patch on the bridge of his nose and black circles under his eyes, he felt like all eyes were on him. He wanted to go back to his B&B to rest, but didn't even want the landlord to see him.

He needed solitude. Evening was coming and a sea mist was closing in, draping the seafront in a fine curtain of white.

He drove out to the North Pier, parking at the viewing spot. A security van waited near the pier's entrance, but the driver was hunched up inside, legs on the dashboard, staring intently into the flickering screen of his mobile phone.

Slim walked down to the North Pier's entrance and assessed the gate. Temporary, you could climb over, but it would make some noise. At one end was a chain-link door, padlocked shut.

He glanced over his shoulder. No movement from the van.

His lock-pick made short work of the padlock.

Inside, he crouched low as he made his way along the metal walkway installed by the construction company along one side of the crumbling pier, aware that the colours would help camouflage him if the security guard happened to look up.

By the time he was halfway out along the pier's three-hundred-yard length, he could barely make out the van at all, and once he reached the island at the end of the pier, the shore was entirely lost in the sea mist.

He felt almost suffocated as he walked across the small island, the daylight enough to see by but the mist closing in over everything more than a few steps ahead. There was little to see; the island was natural rock but had been covered with a concrete platform surrounded by a low wall on which a handful of derelict buildings stood, their roofs caved in. To his left was an abandoned lifeboat station, its sloping slipway abruptly severed halfway along. Directly in front was a small clocktower seven or eight metres high, the missing clock face leaving a gaping circular hole. To his right was a raised viewing platform, weed-strewn, the stairs' stone banister in broken pieces around his feet. He walked up, went to the edge, looking over at the sea sucking and pushing at the rocks below, the tide high, pressing in around the island as though to squeeze it out of existence.

Something had been significant about this place for Bob.

The clock is ticking.

Slim went back to the clock tower, but the clock face was gone, time gone.

Bob had tried to come out here the day he had disappeared.

Why?

The building nearest to the clock was a tumbledown ruin. Slim was able to prise open the crumbling remains of a door but the inside was a jumble of collapsed roof beams. He saw chairs under there, broken and twisted, perhaps the ghosts of a former restaurant.

One hundred and fifty years old the pier might be, but the plastic chairs dated from a later period, perhaps the seventies or eighties. Slim frowned at the debris, wondering what he was seeing, then backed out, turning to look at the clock tower.

Square, a couple of metres to a side, an old entrance at the rear—perhaps for maintenance, now bricked up. The only way inside through the gaping hole where the clock face had been.

The walls, stone, were vertical, offering no handholds. With a pickaxe he could probably break in through the bricked-up entrance, but he had no tools with him. And what was he expecting to find inside? Bob's body? It was the obvious place to hide one, too obvious. The only problem being the tower's height, and to get up to the entrance where the old clock face had been you would need a ladder or at least a grappling hook and rope.

He looked around, searching for something that might work. Back by the old building he fished a broken metal chair leg out of the wreckage.

It took a few minutes to chip away enough old mortar to start levering at the bricks. By the time he had broken a small hole, his back was drenched with sweat.

Certain he was about to discover something significant, he chipped and levered with greater ferocity, his heart racing. A second brick came away, then a third. When a fourth fell, he had made a space big enough to peer inside.

He pulled out a torch and flicked it around the dark space inside. His heart fell, his shoulders slumping. Nothing but a rusted ladder hanging loose from one wall, and some debris on the ground: a couple of seabird skeletons, some leaf litter that must have blown inside, a couple of beer cans thrown through the hole where the clock face had been.

No body, no vital clue that would break the case open.

Disappointed, Slim replaced the bricks as best he could, then took a step back. He surveyed the repaired hole for a moment, then turned and walked back across the courtyard to the wall, peering down into the water on the other side. High tide now, the water sucking and churning below the wall, the current vicious as it drove around the jutting island and east up the Bristol Channel. A far better place to hide a body, in that surging crush of water.

If Bob had gone in there, intentionally or not, he might not ever be found.

31

'IT TOOK me a while but I got something,' Don said. 'I was just trawling data, looking for a break, and I found one of sorts. You're not going to find any family for your guy, I'm pretty sure of that.'

'Bob?'

'He was a ward of the court, put up for adoption in 1962 at the age of three. He was never formally adopted though, and spent his childhood being passed between foster homes and institutions.'

Slim sighed. 'His parents?'

'Only his mother was listed. Anne Sylvia Harker. I tracked her down. Fifteen at the time of Bob's birth. I'm afraid she was dead and buried by twenty. I've found nothing other than a death certificate. Suicide. You probably don't need me to fill in the gaps, Slim.'

'Any other living relatives?'

'None that I can find. No mention of the sister that your contact mentioned. It's possible his mother had other children, but I've found no record of them. Looks like the guy was pretty alone in life.'

'I'm getting that impression. Thanks, Don.'

He hung up. So Bob had no known family, and Reggie's claim that he had a sister looked false. No one would come looking for him; no one would pressure the police to keep working the case. Bob and the woman in his bedroom would slowly fade away, yet another cold case left unsolved.

Slim found a café and ordered coffee. He needed to think, needed to order his thoughts. Bob was missing, possibly dead, possibly on the run. There had been a dead woman in his bedroom, one for whom he had likely been purchasing marijuana as pain relief.

What did Slim know about Bob himself? No family. A Falklands veteran, medically discharged. One who went missing after Goose Green and was later discovered in an Argentine hospital on the mainland.

Reggie had claimed Bob had been doing the Punch and Judy show on the beach for more than fifty years. Slim frowned. That timeframe pre-dated the Falklands War, and would have made Bob a teenager when he took up his beachfront occupation.

Reggie's story clearly didn't add up. There were elements of truth, but too much of it was an obvious fabrication. Reggie himself had been in prison until 2013. Slim sighed, frustrated at his own inability to corroborate witness claims. He was always too willing to follow a rumour, and it had got him in trouble in the past.

It might be worth paying Reggie another visit. Slim paid for his coffee and left, walking up the promenade. When he reached Reggie's place, he found it was already too late for visitors and he was told by a nervous receptionist to come back in the morning.

Aware his broken nose was bringing him unwanted attention, he headed back to his B&B. There, he called

Kay for an update on the Esperanto found on the scraps of paper.

'As I said before, it looks like the scraps of a hand-written novel,' Kay told him. 'Quite why anyone would write it in Esperanto is beyond me, but that's what it looks like. Was this man of yours much of a writer?'

Slim didn't know, but now that he thought about it, Bob must have been following some kind of script for his puppet shows.

'I'm not sure,' he said. 'The man was a puppeteer. I don't know much about what that entails.'

Kay chuckled. 'Well, I did a little reading on your behalf,' he said. 'You said these pieces of paper were being used to make Punch and Judy characters. Is that right?'

'As far as we could tell.'

'Do you think you could find out which character they related to, or better still, get me some of the puppets?'

'I can try, but I don't follow.'

'You see, the lines I've translated vary quite significantly in content,' Kay said. 'There's one here that says "I did my best that day, controlling what I needed to say, swallowing down my pride". But then you've got another that says, "The darkness closes in and all I feel is the pain in knowing that a man is dead because of me"'.

'Wait … what?'

'If this is some kind of first-person novel, then the central character is on quite a varied path, Slim.'

'They sound like confessions.'

'That's what I thought. As though the person was jour-naling his feelings, but first translating them to keep them secret.'

'But what about the puppets?'

'You need to familiarise yourself with the story, Slim. Mr Punch is the main character, along with his wife, Judy.

She tends to berate him for his mistakes and in turn he beats her with his stick. There are other recurring characters too, such as their baby, a policeman, sometimes a crocodile. Then there are the less common characters that used to historically appear, but do so less frequently now, or on the puppeteer's whim. These can include a dog, a horse, a ghost, even a devil.'

'A devil … there was a character we saw who could have been….'

'You might want to get a hold of that one, Slim. And if you can, I'd like to take a look.'

32

'Hey.'

'Are you all right?'

There was a long pause before Chris answered. 'Yeah. I'm all right. Granddad wants your blood, though. It's best if you don't come round.'

'What about my money?'

'I imagine it's gone already.'

Five hundred in an envelope and a phone call from a lawyer that had cost more, and Slim was off the hook. Karen had quipped that he must have been a cat in a former life.

'I'd stay the hell away from my house,' Chris continued. 'Granddad put an old rounders bat just inside the door.'

'Thanks for the heads up. I'm not worried about your granddad though. I'm worried about you.'

'I'm fine. Look, I've still been doing that stuff you asked. It's pretty easy to get out when Granddad sleeps all day. Can I meet you?'

'I'll pick you up. Just tell me where.'

~

AN HOUR later they sat facing each other in a 24-hour McDonald's just off the M5. Chris had a bruise on the side of his left eye, a few days old.

'A frying pan,' he said with a shrug and a grin, as though expecting Slim to find it funny. 'It would have missed but I'd left the dresser cupboard open and I backed into it. The police gave him a rollicking, though, officially put him under caution. That nice one, PC Tasker, she offered me a spot in a hostel.'

'You took it?'

Chris shook his head. 'He's still me granddad. I'm all he's got. He'd drink himself to death if I wasn't watering it down. He told them he'd change, blamed the sauce.'

'People don't change.'

'Didn't you?'

Slim grimaced. 'Maybe, only on the outside.'

'You shouldn't think so low of people. Nor yourself.'

'What changed your tune?'

Chris gave a sheepish grin. 'Believe it or not, you did. Not had no one look out for me before.'

'I didn't do a very good job of it.'

'At least you tried. You looked the part, at least until Granddad nutted you.'

'I'm ex-Armed Forces. I was the part once.' Slim shrugged. 'Once,' he repeated with a wry smile.

'Perhaps you could give me some pointers sometime?'

'In lieu of payment?'

'Are you planning to pay me?'

Slim shrugged. 'Eventually. I always pay my debts ... in the end.'

'Well, I managed to find a couple of people on that bus to Bristol. One said they'd been on the lash the night before and was half asleep the whole way, but the other said she remembered seeing Bob.'

Slim sat up. 'She saw him?'

'Not from the front, as she was a few seats back, but he had this big pack thing with him, like a big canvas bag, which took up the whole seat in front. She remembered noticing because everyone else put their gear under the bus, but just Bob had this big bag thing on the seat. She said she got off behind him, and watched him go along the line of bays and into the toilet at the end.'

'Did she see him come out?'

'She said she got picked up, so didn't wait around.'

Slim frowned. There was no camera that covered the toilet entrance.

'Did you contact the driver?'

'Yeah. He said he didn't remember. Too long ago.'

'That doesn't help us much.'

Chris reached into his bag and pulled out a tatty folder.

'What's that?'

'Me geography file. I hid all this stuff in my school books so Granddad wouldn't see it.' He pushed some print-outs of photographs across the table. 'See these? You know you said you found that dead woman? Is this her?' He jabbed a finger at a figure sitting on a deckchair to the side of the picture. In the centre was Bob's portable theatre, the picture slightly angled as though the camera had been held by a child. The woman was a little out of focus, but it was clear from the angle of her chair that she was watching the show, her hands raised as though to offer applause.

'I don't—' Slim began, but Chris pushed the picture aside to reveal another. Slim had seen it before, but now Chris pointed at a peripheral figure, slightly out of focus, only half in the frame, the left side of her body as she faced away from the camera sliced off.

'You can't see her face,' Slim said.

'Same sandals,' Chris said, pointing at the one visible foot.

'You can't even tell those are sandals.'

'Same colour,' Chris said. 'Close enough. What is it you say? Leap of faith? And here she is again.'

Another picture, another peripheral figure. A woman, facing away, but this time holding something in her hands: an upturned cap.

'These pictures are from three separate summers,' Chris said. 'That enough coincidence for you?'

'That hat—'

'I emailed the woman who posted that picture.' He grinned. 'She replied.'

'And?' Slim didn't want to sound desperate, but couldn't help it as he leaned forward over the table.

'She said the woman was collecting money after the show.'

Slim gave a slow nod. After last speaking to Kay, he had done a little reading up on the history of Punch and Judy.

'A bottler,' he said. 'The puppeteer is known as the professor, with the assistant who collects the money called the bottler. Did they speak to her?'

'Yeah. She said she sounded foreign. Slight twang to her voice. Maybe Spanish. That's her, isn't it? The woman you found in his house?'

Slim gave a slow nod, but his heart was beating so fast that for a moment he couldn't bring himself to speak.

'Not Spanish,' he said at last. 'Ar … Argentinian.'

33

'IT'S QUITE AN ASSUMPTION,' Karen said, sipping a coffee across the table from Slim in the beachfront café. The rain had stopped sheeting across the beach and there was even a hint of blue sky among the clouds. 'I mean, sure, there's the Falklands connection, but it's quite a punt to claim this woman was Argentinian. Do you have any evidence at all?'

Slim shook his head. 'Not yet. But I have a feeling.'

'That's nice and everything, but it's not really practical,' Karen said. 'I mean, even if you're right, how would you find out? Unless she's some sort of international criminal, there's no way to identify her. You can't just ring up the Argentine police and ask for a list of missing persons. Governments would have to get involved.'

'It's a lead, at least.'

'But it doesn't help us find Bob, or what happened to him.' Karen smiled. 'Your nose is looking better. I kind of like the way it angles to the side.'

'That's a trick of the light. And it looked like that before.'

'Maybe I just wasn't paying attention.'

They shared a smile, and Slim felt a momentary urge to ask her to extend their coffee meeting to dinner, but when so many other words would come, those failed him, and the moment passed. Karen sipped her coffee while Slim watched a boy chasing a kite across the beach.

'Any other leads?' Karen asked.

'I found out that Bob used to take in students from Bristol, but that the last was about five years ago and perhaps ended acrimoniously. My guess is that Bob needed the space to allow this woman to move in.'

'It would make sense. Have you tracked down any of these students, in particular the last one?'

'I've got Chris looking into it.'

'How's it going with him?'

'He's a good kid. Dealt a tough hand. I know how that feels.'

'So you've taken him on as a charity case.'

Slim shrugged. 'I needed help, and he was willing. If I can give him a bit of ambition, that's all good. He might even become a cop. You need a few more round here.'

'Budgets, budgets, budgets,' Karen said with a sigh.

'Oh, and I need to get back into the house. There are some belongings of Bob's that I want to take a look at.'

'You're asking this time?'

'What?'

'You were caught on camera the other night.'

'I was…?'

Karen lifted an eyebrow. 'Not so subtle, Slim. It's still a potential crime scene. I had to … archive that video. Luckily no one much cares. I think it might be better for me to go with you next time. Make it official. And we'd better get a move on. It turns out that Bob's place was a council let. We have about a month before his stuff gets moved to storage and the house is cleaned out for a new tenant.'

'A let?'

'He didn't own it, although he'd been in there for years. I don't have access to the social records but he was likely in a vulnerable position.'

'Can you get them?'

'Not without jumping through some hoops.'

'Don't worry, I know a man who's good at that.'

'Well, that's a relief. Let me put in an official request to access the house. It'll only take a day or so.'

'Thanks.'

They went their separate ways. Slim headed back towards his B&B, but had to pass the Grand Pier on the way. He stopped at the fish 'n' chips booth to grab some chips, staring at the space beside him where Karen might have been standing with something like regret.

'Mike, isn't it?'

He looked up as Richard Hardberry passed him the open bag of chips. 'Did you find Bob Harker in the end?'

Slim shook himself awake and focused. 'Still looking, I'm afraid. You haven't heard anything on the rumour mill, I don't suppose?'

'Nothing. It's still pretty quiet at this time of year, though.'

'Must be bad for business.'

Richard shrugged. 'It'll pick up, I'm sure.'

Slim started to turn away, then paused. 'While you've got a moment … would you mind sharing your memories of Bob? Just off the record? It might help with a little background.'

'Ah, sure.' Richard scratched his head. 'He was friendly if you saw him, but never excessively so. A quiet man … I sometimes felt—and I think a lot of people did—that he lived through his puppets.'

'Why's that?'

'Well, there were always rumours about him.'

'What kind?'

'That he had some of mental issue. PTSD, something like that. I heard rumours that he was in the Falklands, also that he was homeless for a while. It looked like he'd straightened himself out, but there were signs, you know.'

'What signs?'

Richard shifted, looking uncomfortable. 'I've never told anyone this, but I found him once, sitting down on the beach, not far from here.' He turned and pointed. 'Just up the promenade there. It was a slow night; I was just stretching my legs.'

'What was he doing?'

'Just sitting on the sand, head in his hands, crying his eyes out.'

'Crying?'

'Yes. Like he had all the troubles in the world. Could have been anything; I didn't stop to ask. A man's tears are his own private thing.'

Slim nodded. 'When he was down on the beach, doing his show, was he always alone? Didn't he have someone collecting money for him?'

'I can't say that I recall. To be fair, if it was busy enough for him to get a crowd, I was probably busy up here. A couple of times, maybe, I saw him with someone, usually some local kid who'd wander the crowd for a couple of quid. Really, though, I wouldn't know. I certainly never saw him with anyone on a regular basis.'

'Thanks for your time.'

'By the way, what happened to your nose?'

Slim smiled, then nodded at the nearest set of promenade steps. 'I tripped. I suppose I'm not used to the wind round here.'

Richard laughed. 'It's caught out many an unsuspecting tourist. You take care.'

'Thanks.'

'See you around.'

Slim left Richard and headed back to his B&B. There he called the local bus company, and was able to speak with Tim, the bus driver who had seen Bob with the man with the crooked finger, but he couldn't recall ever seeing Bob with anyone else, not least an older woman who spoke with a foreign accent.

Tired from hours of trudging around town and a little frustrated that nothing was really taking off, he sat at the small desk in the room and began going through his emails. There was nothing of significance, but he had received a reply from Robert Tiller, this time telling him in no uncertain terms that he had no intention of talking about Jackie Ackerman. Slim wondered if it was a lead he could let go since Reggie's past perhaps had little relevance to Bob's disappearance and possible murder, but he decided to do some online searching anyway, and soon found himself listening to an internet radio show where a former gang member was talking about their past. Tired, Slim was nodding off to sleep when he heard Ackerman's name.

He sat up, ran the segment back a little, and played it again.

'...sometimes karma catches up with you, you know. I knew this guy, Jackie Ackerman. Cocksure, thought he was a lad. Part of getting away with the life requires you to blend in, keep your head down. The kids getting caught, they're just the runners, the nobodies. The higher ups, no one ever sees. Jackie, he had all the goods but he just couldn't keep his mouth shut, you know? One day he sees some guy on the street we used to pick up from time to time. Jackie can't resist a word, a little dig. The guy pulls out a knife and puts it in Jackie, like. And Jackie's dead because he couldn't shut his mouth.'

Slim listened through the rest of the show but the mention of Ackerman had been anecdotal. Slim searched online for the speaker, Larry Amiss, but to his dismay found that the show was a couple of years old, and that Larry had died of liver cancer just six months ago. Slim emailed the host of the radio show anyway, but doubted there was much the man could tell him that hadn't been broadcast.

It might be worth trying to talk to Reggie again, but Slim was reluctant after the last time. Thinking there was little more he could do that night, he decided to take a shower and turn in.

He had just taken off his shirt when his phone rang.

'Karen?'

'Slim?' She sounded frantic. 'Sorry to call so late, but we have a problem.'

'What is it?'

'Someone torched Bob's place. I'm heading out there now.'

'What?'

'I'm pretty sure it's arson, but we won't know right away.'

'I'll meet you there,' he said, pulling his shirt back on.'

'Something else. Was it your idea to put it out on social media that Bob Harker is wanted for murder?'

34

Slim had to wait behind the police tape with the rest of the people gaping, but Karen, out of uniform, spotted him and pulled him aside. Even from across the street, the heat from Bob's burning house tickled his skin. Flames roared from the broken upstairs windows as the fire brigade, only a few minutes ahead of Slim, made it their priority to prevent the fire's spread along the terrace. Along the vaguely erected safety line other residents, some in dressing gowns and pyjamas talked in hysterically loud voices about what had happened, while others argued that it was deserved, that Bob was a murderer, that their only regret was that he had not been inside.

'You can't beat vigilante justice,' Karen hissed, pulling Slim into a garden further up the street. 'Tell me this had nothing to do with you.'

'Of course not.'

'I want to believe you, Slim, but Jesus Christ. We really didn't need this. I've got my superiors spitting bricks at me—'

'What do you mean, vigilante justice?'

'You're not big on computers, are you? Someone posted on a local forum site that Bob was wanted for murder and kidnapping. We've had local reporters ringing the station for the last hour. Tomorrow it'll be all over the news, and it might even make the nationals.' She nodded towards the house where the fire brigade was beginning to bring the blaze under control. 'My guess is that someone round here doesn't like the idea of living near to a murderer.'

'Do you know who posted the claim?'

'No idea. It was posted by an IP hidden behind a VPN, so we can't trace it. The username was CB Radio. It was the first and so far only post by that user.'

'Right.'

'The user posted information known only to the police,' Karen said. 'That's technically a crime. If they pin it on you, at best I'll have to cut you loose.'

'Nothing to do with me.'

'I hope not. But you know who, don't you?'

Slim grimaced. 'I have to make a phone call.'

He moved out of Karen's earshot and took his phone out of his pocket. Chris answered on the second ring.s

'Do you know what you've done?'

Chris gave a nervous laugh. 'Kicked a hornets' nest, just like you suggested.'

'Chris Butler radio. They'll figure it out. I'll do what I can to get you off with a caution. But off the record, I'm proud of you. It's the kind of thing I no longer have the nerve to do.'

'If he's out there hiding somewhere, it'll flush him out. It might be a good idea to have officers alerted at all trans-port hubs in the region in case he tries to run.'

'I'll make that suggestion to PC Tasker. Now, you

should go to bed, and when you get up in the morning, get on with your exam revision.'

'Yes, sir.'

Slim gave a grim smile as he hung up, then headed back to Karen, wondering whether to give her an outright lie or just a little bending of the truth.

35

'Don, it's me.'

'Good morning, Slim. The sun's shining here. How is it for you?'

'Overcast, threatening rain.'

Don laughed. 'I thought it might be. What do you need?'

'NHS records for Bob Harker. I want to know if he was undergoing any psychiatric treatment. There are a couple of local private practices too, if you have any way of hacking those.'

'That's a tough one, but I'll try.'

'Thanks, Don.'

Slim walked into the town centre. Karen had warned him to keep his head down, but as he passed a newsagent, he saw a couple of headlines that would certainly rile her up. *Police hunt local killer. Decomposed body of elderly woman found in house of local Punch and Judy man. Punch and guilty: the seaside entertainer with a dark secret.*

He couldn't help but smile. More eyes were on the case than ever before.

On the downside, the house had been gutted. Old carpets, old furniture, none reaching modern health and safety standards. The place had gone up like a tinderbox, and all that was left was the walls and part of the roof. The houses either side had been evacuated and it was possible all three might need to be demolished.

'Nothing on our cameras,' Karen told him. 'Someone with a really good aim threw an old school Molotov cocktail right through the upstairs bedroom window. The stair carpet caught, and that spread the fire to the downstairs. No trace of petrol nor other flammable substances have been found downstairs, so it's possibly just a chance arsonist, some local punk. We won't know unless a witness comes forward.'

'If Bob's alive and holed up somewhere, this could draw him out,' Slim said.

'Only if he reads the newspapers.'

The rain came as he reached the Grand Pier. He ducked inside for some shelter, then bought a coffee from a booth and headed upstairs. On a Thursday, the gaudy café was mercifully quiet, only a few old couples and some schoolkids doing exam revision.

His phone rang. Chris had come up with a list of students who might have lodged with Bob. Slim had left his laptop in the B&B but thanked Chris and promised to check later.

With a sigh, he pulled out the letter that had arrived for him this morning at the B&B, from the DNA website.

This was the game changer. If he had a match for the mystery woman's DNA, he might be able to identify her and finally unravel the mystery of her presence in Bob's house. And with that, he might be able to figure out where Bob had gone.

He used the end of a teaspoon to prise the envelope

open, then slid out the folded sheet of paper. Turning it over, he took a deep breath before scanning the contents.

'No match,' he muttered aloud. 'Damn it.'

He put the letter back into his rucksack and sipped his coffee. He was used to setbacks, of course, but this one hurt. He had banked on this, and for it to come up short was like a knife in the gut.

For the first time in a while he felt like a beer. His hands began to tremble at the memory, and he gripped the edge of the table to steady himself, squeezing his eyes shut.

'Are you all right?'

He opened his eyes and looked up. Fiona stood nearby, holding a takeaway coffee. 'I know the coffee's pretty rough here and all....'

Slim shook his head. 'Bad day at the office.'

'And it's not even lunchtime. If you want some cheering up, why don't you come into the theatre and watch Amanda screaming at the actors. It's better than EastEnders.'

Slim nodded. 'Sure.'

He followed Fiona into the theatre. She led him into the seating area, and they sat in the dark at the back, watching the group rehearse under the spotlights on the stage. He saw Amanda Smart immediately, standing in the walkway in front of the stage. With a dramatic flap of her arms, she slammed a bunch of papers down on the stage.

'Did you actually read the script?' she snapped at the young man crouching nearby. 'Do it again. It's not too late for anyone to be replaced.'

'Is she always this fierce?' Slim whispered to Fiona.

'You'll see worse if you stick around. She's an utter dragon. It comes from knowing she's the top dog. On the other hand, they have a fixed date for the streaming broadcast and they're nowhere near ready. One of the stagehands called in with flu this morning, which got her back up. And he's the boyfriend of that girl there in the green dress—Lizzie, she's called; she's the one who wrote the script—and she keeps nipping out to call and check he's okay. Only about twenty minutes ago Amanda threatened to kick them both off the production. Honestly, they should be filming this. It would make great TV.'

'I don't doubt it.'

Fiona was silent for a couple of minutes as Amanda put the actors through their paces, then leaned over to Slim and whispered, 'So Bob Harker knocked off some woman, did he? I always thought he was a bit creepy. One of those people who's like a pillar of the community by day but a serial killer by night. Did you know it all along?'

'It's misinformation,' Slim said. 'Just gossip.'

'Are you sure?'

'Was there really a body in his house?'

'Yes, but she died of natural causes. The police are yet to identify her.'

'You know, I saw him with a woman a couple of times.'

Slim sat up. 'You did?'

'Yes. She was much older, and I remember she walked with a cane. I just thought it was his mother. I never got close enough to take a good look.'

'When was this?'

'I don't remember now. Last summer, maybe. I saw her walking with him once, then another time sitting nearby while he did one of his performances. I didn't think anything of it at the time.'

'The police think he was looking after her, but we can't identify her. She had no DNA link to Bob and no one on the missing persons register matches her description. All we know is that she was at least eighty years old and had a Latino accent.'

'I couldn't say I got close enough to hear her speak, I'm afraid.'

They both lapsed into silence. On the stage below, the actors worked through a shipwreck scene with the lead actor begging forgiveness from a spectral Punch and Judy man for some past sin. Slim might have enjoyed it more had Amanda Smart not hollered at one or other of the actors every couple of lines. After a couple of minutes he made his excuses and headed outside.

The rain had stopped and a few spots of blue peeked through the threatening clouds.

He was walking along the promenade when he heard a voice behind him call his name. He turned, and there stood Reggie Bowles, leaning over a broom that looked more like a prop than for any particular use.

'They found him yet?'

'Hey, Reggie. No, I'm afraid not.'

'Not looking in the right place, are they?'

'I don't think so. Don't give up hope.'

'What happened to your face? Someone whack you?'

'A car door—' Slim began, but Reggie's broom had clattered to the ground and his fists had come up. As Slim watched, he bobbed and weaved, throwing out shadow punches as though trying to take out the ghosts of his past.

'Gotta keep your hands up, keep your hands up,' Reggie puffed. 'Don't drop your guard. Then, boom, boom! You take your shot.'

'You used to box, Reggie?'

Reggie was quickly tiring. He threw a weak right hook then stopped, folding to his knees, breathing hard, his eyes squeezed shut. He shook, his breath coming in short, sharp gasps, and Slim realised he was crying.

'Only … only when they made me. And I fought, I did, and I kept my guard up, kept my guard up, but he was big,

and I tried, I tried to stay up, tried for my pride, but he …
he came in, and he hurt me … he … hurt me.'

Slim sighed. He remembered now that Reggie had
been in prison. While his own nine-month stretch for
manslaughter had been sedate and mostly routine, he had
witnessed a couple of fights at a distance. One had been
broken up quickly, but the other had been savage, one man
ending up losing an eye.

'It's all right, you're out of there now. You can put
prison behind you.'

Reggie shook his head. 'Not prison,' he muttered,
barely loud enough for Slim to hear. 'All I have to do is
look up, and I see it, see it, every day. Always there, isn't it?
Always … there.'

'Where, Reggie?'

For a moment Reggie didn't move. Then slowly, like a
broken bird bending itself back into shape, he stood up
straight, lifted an arm, and pointed.

Slim, standing behind him, could see right down the
length of his arm, at where his finger indicated.

The little island at the end of the North Pier.

36

'HE SHOWED UP, Slim. While I don't approve of your methods, they're certainly effective.'

'Not my idea, but I'll take the credit. Where?'

Karen smiled. 'A man matching Bob's description was caught on CCTV at Portsmouth Bus Station last night. We were notified by British Transport Police.'

'You haven't told them that the rumour about Bob being a murderer is false?'

Karen shrugged. 'We've neglected to mention it so far.'

'Can I get a copy of the footage?'

'Sure. I'll send you the file. We've got plain-clothed officers at all the transport hubs in the area, including the ferry ports.'

'Passenger manifests?'

'Working on it. However, at this point we're unsure if he was there to take a bus or had just arrived on one. The footage only shows him walking through the bus station.'

'You need more angles.'

'I know. We're trawling them now.'

Slim called Chris. 'How are you getting on?'

'I heard something, but keep it to yourself. There's a takeaway kebab shop on Ludon Street, just past Farrier's Sports Gym. I overheard some guys talking. You didn't hear it from me.'

'I haven't heard anything from you.'

'Go and see.'

'Perhaps it's about time I did some exercise,' Slim said. 'And what better way to celebrate than with a kebab?'

He hung up, then walked across town, preferring to take the time to feel the place, rather than rush through in a car. It also gave him the chance to take a detour past Bob's place, but it was taped off, the windows boarded up. Slim paused for a moment, staring at it with regret, then headed on.

He didn't use the gym, but did at least go into its lobby where he bought a drink from a vending machine and then looked at the posters for a while. Then, checking his watch to see it was close enough to lunchtime, he headed for the kebab place.

A handful of plastic tables and chairs lined a floor-to-ceiling window, but the high counter told him it was predominantly a late-night takeaway spot. He glanced at the menu on the wall overhead, then ordered a coffee and a hamburger for takeaway. As he watched the man lean into the kitchen and shout the order at a kid standing by an industrial-sized griddle, he wondered why Chris had told him to come here.

And then he saw it. As the kid put down his mobile phone and pulled on a pair of plastic gloves, one little finger caught a moment before he adjusted the glove to cover it.

Slim took his burger and coffee to a bench across the street, where he ate while watching the shop. The day was struggling to find any heat and he wished he'd brought a blanket or something as he sat in the cold, hoping the kid was only working part-time and not at the start of an all-day shift.

He had to pace a while, just to keep the cold at bay, but at three o'clock the owner turned the sign on the door to CLOSED and a few minutes later the kid emerged, wearing a hoodie, hands deep in his pockets. Slim fell into step, far enough back not to be noticed, close enough to keep the boy in sight. His temptation was to haul the boy in now, but he wasn't convinced the boy would have much to tell him. After all, he knew why Bob had been buying the weed. He just wanted to know if the boy knew. Perhaps Bob had let slip some mention of the woman, a name perhaps?

He trailed the boy along several streets, then realised he was coming to a familiar part of town. He turned a corner and there was Bob's street in front of him. On the corner, the boy headed straight into the newsagent. Slim waited outside for the boy to emerge, but after fifteen minutes, he decided to go in.

The boy had gone. There was just the old shopkeeper, flipping through a magazine. Slim thought about mentioning the boy, then caught a glimpse into the hall beyond, a cramped space at the foot of a set of stairs.

A pair of shoes lay on their sides at the bottom of the stairs.

Slim bought a chocolate bar and went back out, heading across the street. From there, he could see a light on in the upstairs window.

'Huh.' The boy dealing weed to Slim had been right there, all the time, living in the shop at the end of Bob's street.

37

'I've been working through that list you gave me,' Chris said, a wide grin on his face as he sat across the table from Slim, a hamburger in front of him. 'I slacked off a bit because I wanted to pass my Spanish exam. It's next week.'

'You're going to show up?'

Chris nodded. 'Yeah.'

'What about the others?'

Chris's smile dropped. 'Thinking about it.'

'I would.'

'Did you?'

'Most of them,' Slim said with a smile. 'Just to spit in my teachers' eyes, for the most part. No one thought I'd achieve anything. They were almost right. I got five Cs, enough to get into the army.'

'You were a soldier?'

'First Gulf War. I was eighteen, a kid with an anger problem. I just wanted to work my stress out on the assault courses. I didn't expect to be deployed.'

'Did you see action?'

Slim closed his eyes. Once he had needed to drink to

get over the memory of a pair of boots on the sand, still filled with a pair of human feet. He had learnt to face it, but still couldn't find any words that made sense to describe it.

'Actually,' he said, shrugging it off, 'that's where "Slim" came from. We were unloading some equipment—'

Chris flinched as a bell announced the café door was opening. Slim glanced round as Chris cowered, saw a group of lads come in, among them a couple Slim recognised from the park near Bob's place.

As one spotted Chris, the air turned hostile.

'Hey, C, how's your new friend?'

A couple of ringleaders drew the whole group around the table, hoodies, tattoos, pouts and watery, unintelligent eyes. Behind them, another customer swiftly left, while the owner's calls to get out went ignored. Slim counted six; not a fight anyone could realistically win. He took his eyes off them just long enough to risk a glance at Chris, whose eyes had gone hard as he rose out of his seat, his towering frame giving him a head advantage, even if his frail body swiftly reduced it.

'We're just talking.'

'Is that what you call it? We thought you were one of us, man. What are you, some police snitch?'

'Teach him a lesson, Ace.'

At the nickname, Slim couldn't help smiling.

'What are you laughing at?'

'Ace? What are you, Thunderbirds?'

A couple near the back looked confused, missing the cultural reference. The one called Ace turned towards Slim. He was fat and meaty, the kind of kid who could take a punch and throw one. Slim, still sitting, tried to calm himself. Perhaps he could talk his way out of this.

'You taking the—'

'How about showing that you really are an Ace and walking away?' Slim suggested.

Ace looked about to do just that, but one behind him said something. He turned towards Chris, one fist punching out, catching Chris on the side of the face. As Chris groaned, knees buckling, Slim's vision turned to a red mist. His heart raced, and all he could hear was a loud ringing in his ears.

Beneath the table he kicked a chair opposite him. As its back slammed into Ace's stomach, making him double over, Slim lifted the plastic table with his knee so that it met Ace's face on the way down. As blood sprayed across the Formica, Slim rose to his feet, overturning the table, making space. He grabbed a chair, turning it around, the legs facing outwards.

Ace was on his knees, clutching at his face. Most of the others had backed away to the door, but one kid had something in his hand that glinted silver under the café lights: a screwdriver. As the owner hollered that the police were on their way, Slim edged forward, keeping the chair between him and the kid with the knife.

'I've done time,' Slim said, staring the boy down. 'Prison breaks kids like you. Make the right choice now.'

The kid dropped the knife and ran, following the others as they fled up the street. Slim put down the chair and turned to Ace, still on his knees. As the café owner, brandishing a wooden cudgel came out from behind the counter, Slim squatted beside Ace and put a hand on his shoulder.

'You can get six months for what you just did,' he said, picking a number out of the air. 'Now, we could wait for the police, or we could find somewhere to settle this like men. You like the sound of that?'

Ace, snot and blood bubbling from his nose, shook his head.

'Or you can walk away, and you can stay away from Chris, myself, and this café. If I see you again, I won't ask first. Do you understand me?'

Ace nodded, then shrugged, knocking Slim's arm aside. 'Go.'

Clutching his nose, Ace barrelled out of the door.

'I apologise for the mess,' Slim said to the owner.

'It's an easy clean. That group of punks is the bane of my life.'

'If you have names, I have a friend in the police who'd be happy to have a word. Your cameras working?'

'Yes.'

'Good.' Slim turned to Chris. 'Did he hurt you?'

Chris smiled as he rubbed at a bruise on his cheek. 'Compared to Granddad, he hits like a girl.'

'Does he go to your school?'

'No, he left a couple of years ago.'

'If he comes within sight of you, call me.'

Chris nodded, then offered him a smile, staring at Slim with something like wonder. 'That was like some kind of Chuck Norris move. How did you do that?'

Slim shrugged. 'I got lucky. I had no idea he was so close to the chair. Must be too many kebabs.'

38

AFRAID THE GANG might be hiding out somewhere, he walked Chris back to his house, unable to shake the irony of Chris's home life.

'He hasn't touched me since the police came round,' Chris assured him, even though Slim knew there was no such thing as never with abusive people. He watched Chris go with a heavy feeling in his heart, then turned his focus back to the task in hand because that was the only thing he could do to take his mind off the things he couldn't.

～

'THE BOY'S name's James Jackson,' Karen told Slim over the phone half an hour later. 'He's on our radar. Nineteen years old, already has a caution for possession and two months suspended for a car break-in. He's a small fish, though. We keep tabs on him more for who he might associate with. Want me to bring him in?'

'At this point, I don't think there's much he could help us with. If you could keep an eye on him, though.'

'I'll do what I can. Have you viewed that footage I sent you, yet?'

'I'll look tonight.' Slim sighed. 'Not enough hours in the day.'

'So we use the ones in the night, don't we?'

Slim smiled. 'Sadly so.'

'Oh, by the way, we've collected what was salvageable from Bob's house. There's not much, but it's in a lock-up because the council want to move in and start seeing what they can salvage of the building. I can take you up to have a look if you like.'

'Would tomorrow morning work?'

'Perfect.'

They hung up. Slim went back to his B&B and sat down with his laptop. First, he viewed the video Karen had sent him, but it was grainy, difficult to pick out details. There was Bob, a blurry shape limping down the concourse, difficult to make out, appearing just long enough to be caught on camera, then lumbering out of shot.

And that, Karen had said, was it.

No other footage, no definite sightings of Bob, no passenger lists where his name appeared.

His description had been passed to British Transport Police. Bob, with his limping gait, floppy hat and oversized backpack, couldn't be missed. He would stand out in the biggest of crowds.

Slim sat back. Something wasn't right. Cameras were everywhere these days, yet Bob was appearing just enough to lead the police away.

He didn't have a phone he could download the video to, so he put his laptop in his bag and headed back out. It was getting late, but as he walked along the promenade to the Grand Pier, he saw lights on in some of the shops and stalls near the entrance.

His initial plan had been to call on Reggie, but the care home was closed for the night. Instead he went up to the fish n' chips shop by the entrance and hailed Richard Hardberry.

Remembering Richard still knew him as Mike, Slim spun a story about how his supposed documentary might now be one helping to find the missing Bob. Richard looked at the video clips and nodded.

'It sure looks like him. Is it true he's accused of murder?'

'I can only go on the reports I've read,' Slim said, careful not to give too much away, but feeling a little disappointed inside. 'Your guess is as good as mine.'

'I can't believe it of him. I didn't know him well, but he seemed like a nice man.'

'Looks can be deceiving,' Slim said, feeling like a fraud as he quoted the old cliché.

He headed onward along the promenade, mind buzzing too much to go back to the B&B to sleep. There were a few people about, a couple of dog walkers, a group of rowdy young men spilling out of a waterfront pub. Slim walked all the way along, finding himself at the leisure boat harbour at the northern end, where a handful of small boats bobbed in the water. A couple of men were unloading fishing gear, with one even preparing to go out, even as the last light of the late sunset fell. Slim lifted a hand as the man noticed him and smiled.

'Is it safe to go out there at this time of night?' he asked.

The man grinned. 'Nothing like a bit of night fishing. Not for the faint of heart. You a fisherman?'

Slim still had an old rod somewhere, most likely collecting dust. 'I dabble,' he said.

'Well, from one angler to another, happy fishing,' the man said, unhooking his boat from the mooring post and starting the outboard motor. Slim lifted a hand as the man angled left to avoid a boat on the way in.

Slim turned back to the town, squinting at the lights starting to come on. It was nearly ten o'clock, the sun gone, the sky purple. The town, enjoying the long early summer nights, was only just starting to wake.

The boat came in behind him. Slim glanced back to make sure he wasn't in the way of any mooring efforts, then frowned at the sight of the man in the boat. The man too noticed him, and a look of confusion turned to shock and then to anger.

'What on earth are you doing out here?'

Slim stared at Robert Tiller, the former gangster turned activist, remembering the abruptness of the man's last email rebuttal.

'I could ask you the same thing,' he said, as Tiller glared at Slim with hostile eyes.

39

SLIM BAULKED AT ENTERING A BAR, but the sailing club was at least a little removed from the kind of establishment where he might find the pressure to drink too great. A handful of fishing, boating types sat around, talking garrulously about their day on the water.

'I'm trying to look out for you,' Tiller said, one hand clutching a pint glass. He sounded both nervous and angry. Slim had opted for coffee, but Tiller's drink had spilled and he had to force himself not to dip his fingers into the little puddle and stick them in his mouth. 'I might be out of that scene but there are plenty who aren't. If you ask too many questions, you'll need to start looking over your shoulder.'

'I didn't know you were a fisherman,' Slim said, changing the subject.

'Barely. I like to go out from time to time. Nothing biting tonight.'

'I noticed.'

Tiller grimaced. 'I'm not the best.'

'Didn't know you were local either.'

'Bristol,' Tiller said. 'Local enough. What's that got to do with anything?'

'I just wanted to know about Ackerman. Why he was killed by Reggie Bowles.'

'And I told you, I don't know. And even if I did, I wouldn't tell you, simply for your own protection.'

'I don't need protecting.'

Tiller sighed. 'Men like you always say that. Then they wash up dead.'

'Why wash up? That how you work?'

'What is this, an interrogation?'

'I just want answers. You have them. I know you do.'

'You really want to know about Ackerman? Ackerman was an arsehole. He liked to do a bit of homeless bashing, just for laughs. My guess is he tried it on Reggie, who happened to have a knife on him. Just a guess. That answer your question?'

Slim sipped his coffee. 'It answers one question,' he said. 'But one always leads to another, doesn't it?'

'What do you mean?'

'I checked your schedule. You're active round here, Gloucestershire, Somerset. But you don't go much further afield. For such an outspoken advocate, you don't go far from your old hunting ground.'

'My appearances are voluntary, and you know what petrol prices are.'

Slim shrugged. 'Let's assume that's true for now.'

Tiller glared at him, leaning so far over his drink Slim wondered if he would launch an attack.

'I'm trying to help you,' Tiller growled.

Slim nodded and stood up. 'And I think you have,' he said, turning away and walking to the door, not looking back.

As soon as he was outside, he hurdled a low wall and

crept into a space behind some old boating equipment. As he had expected, a few seconds later Tiller appeared, fists clenched, spoiling for a fight. He stalked up the path outside the sailing club, looking for Slim. At the end of the path, where it exited onto a road, he looked both ways, kicked at a traffic sign in frustration, then headed back into the club.

Slim gave Tiller enough time to settle back into his beer, maybe make some new friends. Then he headed down to the moored boats and searched for Tiller's.

He hadn't seen the man carry anything into the club. And as he shone a torch over the inside of the boat, he couldn't see anything else inside either.

Tiller was either lying, or he liked to go fishing with his hands.

40

'THERE'S NOT MUCH,' Karen said as she led Slim into a storeroom that smelled of smoke. Mostly a few tins. The fire started on the upper floor so all his clothing was destroyed. We salvaged a little from downstairs but the floor collapsed and there wasn't much left.'

Slim squatted down to look at the plastic crates of mostly charred items. Some were recognisable—a whole crate of fire-damaged crockery, a couple of empty picture frames, the corner of a plastic holder with part of a calendar sticking out—while other crates just carried piles of ashes.

Slim turned to one which contained charred lumps of paper. 'These,' he said. 'These were his puppets?'

'I believe so. Some have wire inserts, probably to move them around.' Karen shrugged. 'I'm not too knowledge-able about such things, I'm afraid.'

Slim scooped one out and peeled away a few blackened shreds of paper until he found one that contained a few lines of text in what Kay told him was Esperanto. There was no way to identify the puppet; three quarters had been burned. All that was left seemed to be a solid lump, maybe of wood, that made up the head, with a few scraps around the outside.

Almost nothing, but if there was anything left of interest, Kay would find it.

'What's that?' Karen asked. 'It looks like Spanish.'

Slim considered how much to tell her, although they were supposed to be on the same side.

'I think it's gibberish,' he said. 'Maybe the kind of fake paper sold in craft shops. I have a linguist friend, however. I can ask him to take a look.'

'Sure. There's no way I could get clearance for anything like that. Make sure you log what you take with me.'

～

AN HOUR LATER, a box of charred puppets was on its way to Kay by express courier. Slim stepped out of the parcel company's office, feeling like an idiot. What could he hope to possibly find from a bunch of random scribblings transcribed into a language no one actually used?

He walked down to the seafront to get a coffee. Patches of blue made a quilt out of the grey, and to his surprise, a group of kids were playing in the sea. He tried calling Chris but got no answer, so instead opened his laptop and got to work trying to track down the list of students who had lodged at Bob's place. There were more than twenty names on the list, but luckily most aspired to the modern social media generation and were easy to find online. Many of them hadn't even set their profiles to private, so before contacting any, he browsed what photos and videos he could find, getting a sense of who the people were. It seemed Bob had favoured students in the arts; one was now a journalist in London, another was a painter with an online shop. A couple had moved overseas, while one or two still lived locally. Slim smiled at one who was into costuming, then found himself surprised to see the young man standing against a backdrop of the very beach outside the café window. Slim looked for the date the photo was posted, but while he was still trying to figure out how to display it, his phone buzzed on the tabletop.

'Chris?'

'Sorry I didn't get your call. I was in an exam.'

'How did it go?'

Chris chuckled. 'We'll see. Geography. Not my best subject, but I had a decent crack.'

'Good for you. Everything else all right?'

'So far, so good. Listen, I meant to call you this morning, but I forgot to charge my phone. I found her.'

'Who?'

'The woman living in Bob's place. I found her.'

41

'I THOUGHT I'd practice my Spanish, right? I went searching for missing persons websites from Argentina. It took some hunting around, but I found her. Maria-Luisa Gonzalez. She disappeared in 2014, thought to have left the country. And get this. She was a retired nurse.'

Slim could barely bring himself to reply. In a stunned stutter he asked Chris to email him all the details. Fifteen minutes later he had the woman's face on the screen in front of him.

Maria-Luisa Gonzalez, born in 1940, from Rio Gallegos, Argentina. The information had been posted by her son. Feeling like he was inside some kind of surreal cloud, Slim wrote a message and translated it online. Then he posted it to the listing.

By the time he had ordered another coffee, a reply had come. An hour later, Slim found himself back in his bedroom at the B&B, reading an email from Marco-Thomas Gonzalez, Maria-Luisa's son.

.   .   .

DEAR MR HARDY,

Your message was one most welcome in our family, although one for which we are still dealing with our grief. That it appears my mother was cared for in her final days was something of a consolation. We look forward to a confirmation being made of my mother's identity and thank you for your offer to work with the police to make a formal identification possible. Your description and the photographs bear such likeness to my mother that I am sure this is just a formality.

Thank you for your questions. I will try to answer them as best I can.

My mother vanished on 31st January, 2014. For some years since her retirement from nursing she had been involved in local politics, an outspoken critic of our regional government to the point where she had begun to fear for her life. There was an incident a few weeks before her disappearance in which my mother's car was set alight. We never discovered if it was due to petty crime or something larger, but we believe it was the catalyst for my mother's disappearance. She left no note, only took her passport and some cash, and vanished. The authorities could not trace her. We believed she went over the border into Bolivia but we never received word, nor learned what happened to her.

While it is some consolation to know of her whereabouts, it is also something that fills us with grief. For your contact we are grateful, and we look forward to hearing from you further.

Yours

Marco-Thomas Gonzalez

42

FROM THE LOOKOUT SPOT, Slim watched the North Pier as mist swirled around it, sometimes hiding everything, other times revealing just the island at the end of the old pier as though it floated isolated in the air. Nearby, a couple of photographers leaned over their camera lenses, looking for the perfect shot. On the other side of the road below, a security van waited by the fence, blocking off the pier's old entrance. Even from here, Slim could see the reflection of the security guard's smartphone screen through the side window.

Bob Harker had come here on the day of his disappearance.

Why?

Had he made it onto the pier? If so, where had he gone, and how had he got back to the main beach in time to be seen by Reggie?

Slim stared at the pier until the mist closed in again, hiding it from sight.

He had no idea.

He headed for a meeting with Karen in the town. He

had already passed on the information about the woman's possible identity. The police were now involved in formally identifying her, and if correct, her body would be cremated and her ashes returned to her family.

'We've traced her,' Karen said. 'Maria-Luisa was a nurse at the Rio Gallegos hospital where Bob was flown after being injured at the battle of Goose Green. While we'll likely never know what happened between them, it's almost certain that's where they met. Perhaps Bob felt indebted to her. They must have maintained contact, and when she fled the country, Bob offered to look after her.'

'And he had to kick out the last of his student lodgers at short notice in order to make room,' Slim said.

'It makes sense.'

'He kept her hidden. The garden at the back was for her. I remember seeing some exotic plants; maybe they were to keep her happy when she was too frail to go outside. Before she got sick, she sometimes went down to the beach with him, but they always travelled separately. Maybe Maria-Luisa liked to walk, I don't know. But in public Bob kept her just enough at arm's length that people wouldn't notice.'

'And then she became ill?'

Slim nodded. 'She was a nurse. She might have known. And she also would have known that she could be deported if her identity was revealed. Hence the medicinal marijuana that Bob was procuring from James Jackson. The boy lived nearby; chances were that Bob knew him, at least to speak to.'

'That makes sense too.'

Slim sipped his coffee. 'It does.'

'So where's Bob? Who or what did Reggie see, and why did Bob go on the run?'

Slim smiled. 'You're the policewoman. You tell me.'

Karen rolled her eyes. 'And you're the famous private investigator.'

Slim shook his head. 'Right now, I have no idea. But if that was Bob in Portsmouth Bus Station, you need to bring him in.'

'If?'

'You go with facts. I'll do the speculating.'

'You know what they say about assumptions?'

'I do, and I've been caught out on many occasions. I would go so far to assume anything right now, though.'

'If she died of natural causes, and Bob went on the run, then at worst we have a case of abetting an illegal and corpse abandonment. In the great scheme of things—'

'But Bob doesn't know that. And don't forget, he could be suffering from trauma. He isn't thinking straight.'

'So you think that's him on the footage?'

Slim shrugged. 'Let's assume it is. We need to pull him in, and put this thing to bed.'

'And if it isn't?'

'Then Reggie Bowles comes back into play.'

'Do you really think he saw something that night?'

Slim shrugged. 'I have no idea. I'll go and talk to him again anyway. Last time I saw him he was acting a little strange.'

'Well, just be careful. Your nose looks much better pointing forward.'

Their eyes met for a moment. Slim felt his cheeks redden, a little warmth under his collar. It had been a long, long time. Karen, for her part, seemed to realise his sudden awkwardness and looked away, smiling as she sipped her coffee, looking out over the beach.

'I prefer it that way too,' he muttered at last, wondering why it was suddenly so difficult to think of anything to say.

43

IT WOULD TAKE a few days for Maria-Luisa to be formally identified, and Bob had again gone to ground. Slim changed B&B again, concerned that Robert Tiller might still have a beef with him. This time, he found a place just a street back from the beach, five minutes on foot from the Grand Pier.

He had recently spoken to Kay, who had received the charred remains of Bob's puppets and was now in the process of picking them apart. Chris had gone quiet while he took more of his exams, although he told Slim he had failed to show up for his art exam because, 'you can't really teach that, can you?' Karen was keeping Slim up to date with the police investigation, but the only news was that Bob was yet to be found on any footage, meaning he had vanished again.

May turned to June, and the weather dragged itself towards something comparable with summer. The evenings stretched late into the night and had it not been for the wind off the sea, Slim might have considered leaving his coat in his room during his long, nightly walks along the promenade.

He had little to do other than trawl through lists of names, sending emails, hoping for something that might lead to something else.

The few emails that came back contained a lot of nothing. A student from Bristol University gave Slim a multi-page account of her three months staying with Bob in 2012, during which time nothing of note had happened. A passenger on a bus that might—but might not—have taken Bob to Portsmouth hadn't actually seen him, but had an extensive list of possibilities, with an equally extensive list of conspiracy theory websites where Slim could no doubt find the answers.

Printing and filing everything, Slim was building a significant body of work around the case, but none of it was leading him to the answer he wanted.

Where was Bob Harker?

Chris had kicked the proverbial hornets' nest, briefly blowing the case wide open. Now it had gone quiet again. Karen had complained to Slim about resources being directed elsewhere.

And then Kay called him.

'Slim, I found something.'

'Something on the paper? What does it say? Is it something important?'

'I'm still working through that, but that's not what I meant. I found something else, wrapped up inside. It's a signet ring. I've bagged it, kept it uncontaminated. I really think you need to take a look, particularly in light of what I've found on the paper it was wrapped in, and what I found on it under the microscope.'

'What are you talking about?'

'The paper surrounding it appears to be the shredded

remains of a confession. I guessed from flecks of red paint among the outer ash that this was the devil puppet. The text was all in Esperanto, again, so I translated it as best I could. Slim … I think your guy Bob might have killed someone.'

44

SLIM MET Kay in a small roadside café on the A4 between Bath and Chippenham. It had been some years since they had come face to face and they greeted each other with a warm hug.

'You've lost weight,' Kay said with a grin.

'You've gained it,' Slim answered. 'It's good to see you again.'

'And you. We shouldn't leave it so long next time.'

'For sure. How have you been?'

'Busy. Turning work away.'

'I appreciate you always putting yourself out for me.'

'I wouldn't have it any other way. Most of what I do is drudge work. Pays the bills but it's dull. And then you send me something leftfield. I mean, what the hell is this? Rings wrapped in shreds of handwritten Esperanto text? You can't make this up, Slim.'

'I wish I had. Let's get some coffee and you can show me what you have.'

They took a window table near the back. Slim ordered the drinks while Kay opened a bag and took out several files and containers. They put their drinks on an adjacent table to remove the risk of spillage, then Kay passed the first file across to Slim.

'These are fragments of translated text. My guess is that he had some kind of diary or perhaps a memoir he was writing. He wrote down his thoughts, then cut them up and used them to build his puppets. Each puppet was an aspect of his personality. This one, for example, appears to have been a jester or perhaps a clown.' Kay took out a photograph of a charred chunk of paper. There were a few flecks of green and yellow in among the ashes. 'I know it doesn't look like much, but bear with me. In the middle of it, I found this.'

He took out a small plastic evidence bag. Inside, still covered with glue residue, was a red plastic nose.

'Huh. It's like one of those charity things,' Slim said.

'You're right. That's exactly what it is. And these are some of the things written on the paper I found wrapped round it.'

'"Tapped a little boy's hat today. The wind caught it and it landed on a little dog. It jumped about three feet in the air. More laughs than my show ever gets."' Slim ran a finger over the text. '"A boy on the promenade asked me if I'd ever seen a camel. I told him only in the mirror, then did my best impression, patting my bag."'

Slim looked up. 'Happy memories,' he said.

'I'll point out now that the translations weren't perfect,' Kay said. 'He wasn't a native. My guess is that he used Esperanto to keep his thoughts secret. Perhaps it was a therapy thing. Maybe he was just a private person. Now take a look at this.'

Kay passed Slim another evidence bag which contained a gold signet ring. Slim frowned at the crest, tainted with age.

'What's that?'

'I looked it up. It's a regimental signet. My guess is these rings were worn by members of Harker's military regiment back in the Falklands War.'

'What's it doing in there? You said this was the remains of the devil puppet? Did he commit some war crime? Perhaps kill someone in combat?'

'It's possible. Something that weighed on his mind so heavily that he condemned himself. Look at these. I translated these from the paper around the ring. Sadly, there were not many left.'

Slim lifted the file Kay had passed him. It contained several sheets of paper with Kay's neat handwriting in short paragraphs with a line space between each one.

'"There are days when it comes back,"' Slim read. '"Days when it's all I see, wherever I look, and I wish the water had swallowed me."'

He looked down the list. Snippets. Fragments of thoughts. The words of a man dealing with the darkest of his demons.

I did what I had to do. When you rush into battle, it's kill or be killed, him or me. But why did it have to be him and not me?

All I can see is him coming forward. It's not rage in his face, but desperation. I'm going to die. I have to fight. I don't want to die. I have to … fight. And I win. And he's dead.

There are men all around, and they want blood. They need blood, or I die. I don't want to die, so he has to. If I could take it back, I would change everything. I would lower my hands, let him come.

The devil rides with me. Every step. He sits there, and he goads me, and he tells me what I did wrong. And sometimes he shows me that man's face, and all the pieces that I've glued together start to come apart.

Slim sighed. It went on and on. Clippings from a man's life, the detail indistinct as though Bob saw it with crystal clarity and needed only to reason with it. To come to terms with its existence.

He looked up at Kay. 'He's talking about the Falklands War,' he said. 'About the combat he saw. It looks like he went hand to hand with someone, and they died.'

Kay nodded. 'That's what I thought too.' He tapped a finger on the evidence bag containing the ring. 'Then there's this. He wanted to bury it, in his way.'

'How so?'

Kay took something from his pocket. A magnifying glass. He held it out to Slim. 'Take a look. It's easier under a lab microscope, but this should be enough.'

Slim peered through the magnifying glass at the ring.

'Look at the insignia,' Kay said.

'It's ... dirty. Is that—'

'It's human tissue. It's skin.'

Slim looked up. 'Good God. The man he killed?'

'Could be. I hope you don't mind, but I took the liberty of taking a sample and sending it off for analysis.' He gave a sheepish shrug. 'I have a mate. Us forensics types tend to stick together.'

Slim nodded. 'Thank you.'

It could mean anything. The man Bob had killed, if they could identify him, perhaps discover a link to Maria-Luisa, to the Falklands War, it might help. Dates were important, Slim knew. Could the day Bob vanished have been the anniversary of his darkest war moment?

They talked for a while longer. Kay passed Slim the other notes he had made so far, from the other remains he had salvaged.

'Don't leave it so long,' Kay said, as they shook hands outside the café and parted ways. 'Take care of yourself, Slim.'

'And you. I appreciate your help, Kay. All of it.'

Almost as soon as he was back in the car, his phone rang.

'Karen?'

'Slim, where are you? There's been a development.'

'I'm out of town but I'm heading back your way now. What happened?'

'We found something on CCTV.'

'Bob?'

'No. His house. We know who torched it.'

Slim's face flushed with heat. The fear that she would tell him it was Chris made it hard to breathe.

'Who?' he asked, voice little more than a croak.

'That kid. James Jackson.'

45

'Can I talk to him first?'

'Slim, this is arson. It's a police matter. We need to bring him in.'

'He won't speak. You know kids like that.'

'He'll be facing a minimum of five years in prison. He'll speak.'

'At best you'll get a line about vigilante justice, that he thought he was doing the community a favour.'

'Maybe he thinks he was.'

'Come on, Karen. It's more than that.'

'You're not above the police, Slim.'

'I know, but—'

'We're sending a car to pick him up. In an hour.'

'Karen—'

'In an hour, Slim.'

She hung up. Slim looked at his watch. It would be tight, but he could make it.

He would need some luck. He pulled into a spot just up the road from the newsagent and jumped out of the car. During the drive he had gone through a number of scenarios for how this might play out.

Now that he was here, none of them seemed realistic. He could barge into the shop, demand to see the boy. Pretend to be a friend—no chance they would believe him. Snatch him off the street—and he could go down for kidnapping.

He was still thinking what to do when the newsagent door opened and the kid came out. He wore a hoodie, hands in his pockets, a backpack on. Head lowered, he was almost past Slim when Slim said, 'I know about Bob Harker.'

The kid looked up, eyes telling Slim all he needed to know. As Jackson turned to run, Slim picked a direction, getting lucky, getting a hand up that Jackson ran into. As the boy tried to wriggle away, Slim caught his wrist and twisted it, using a hold he'd learnt in the army to get control. He pushed Jackson up against the wall, leaning close.

'I'm not police,' he said. 'But they're on their way. If you tell me what I want to know about Harker, I can help you.'

'I don't know nothing—'

'You're on camera. It's clear cut. You torched Harker's place. You supplied him with drugs. He's missing, maybe dead. You have motive. How does twenty to life sound? You know how hard prison is for a kid as young as you?'

'I didn't—'

'You did. Get in the car.'

Jackson stopped struggling. Slim knew the drill. If he let go of the boy, the boy would bolt. He would give chase for a while, but run himself out. He relaxed his grip a little, waiting for the inevitable. To his surprise, Jackson said, 'You were in Pete's Eats the other day. I made you a kebab.'

Slim smiled. 'It was a good kebab.'

'Thanks.'

'The police are on their way. You can talk to me, James, or we can wait for them.'

Jackson relaxed, but he still shook his head. 'I needed the money, man. Mum's shop ... the rates went up. I—we —needed the money.'

'You're going to work now? Let me give you a lift. You don't have to say anything.'

Jackson sighed. 'All right.'

Slim twisted the boy around, then let him go. He tensed, still expecting the boy to run, but he had got as much assurance as he could expect. He watched Jackson take a couple of steps towards the car.

'This it?' he muttered, shaking his head. 'What a heap. I was hoping it was that Lexus up the street.'

'Just get in and shut up.'

'They say crime don't pay. Doesn't look like being in with the pigs pays well either.'

As Jackson pulled open the door, climbed in and disdainfully slammed the door after him, Slim actually smiled.

46

Slim took a scenic route, out to the suburbs. He expected to hear sirens in the distance but none came.

'How long were you supplying Harker with drugs?'

Jackson shrugged. 'A year. He started coming in the shop, buying all the ibuprofen, the paracetamol. Mum was worried he was going to off himself. One day I asked him if he wanted something; I could sort him something stronger. Said it as a joke, like. He looked at me, asked how much.'

'And it went on from there?'

'Yeah. As time went on, he wanted harder and harder stuff.'

'What were you selling him?'

'Started off just weed. Then he wanted prescription stuff. Painkillers. As strong as I could get.'

'It was good money for you.'

'Yeah.'

'You were bitter that he disappeared, that you lost a customer? Is that why you torched his place?'

'Nah, man. Don't put words in my mouth.'

'Did you fall out?'

'The last time I saw him he said he was done. Didn't say why. I didn't see him after that.'

'And you were angry?'

'Nah, man. I got other customers.'

'You burned Bob Harker's place. Why?'

Jackson pressed back in the seat, staring straight ahead. Slim took another turning, heading out into the country-side, the town behind them. He waited, hoping James would talk without prompting. It was always the best way, to give the person a silence they would eventually feel compelled to fill.

Finally, just as Slim was about to crack and offer another question, Jackson said, 'He'll kill me, man.'

'I'm not the police. I work with them, sometimes against them. Nothing you tell me needs to go further, but if it helps me to find Bob Harker … you were paid, weren't you?'

A barely perceptible nod.

'Who?'

Silence. Slim waited for a few moments, then said, 'The same guy who supplies the drugs? The same guy who … broke your finger?'

A tear beaded in the corner of Jackson's eye as he dipped his head and looked away.

'The dashboard,' Slim said, pointing at the front of the car. 'Write it. Just a name. That's all I want. Give me that, and I can give you a chance.'

Jackson did nothing for a long time. Then at last he reached up, only his crooked finger visible from the end of his cuff. With tears in his eyes, he began to trace out words, his mouth moving at the same time, the words that tumbled free as light and frail as a dying wind.

Slim stared, disbelieving.

47

NOT A NURSE, but a psychiatrist. Maria-Luisa Gonzalez had worked as a psychiatric nurse in the hospital where Bob had been taken. Bob, traumatised by his battlefield injuries and experiences, had remained in the hospital for nearly four months before reduced hostilities and the easing of diplomatic tensions had allowed him to be flown back to the UK.

During that time, he had been placed under the supervision of Maria-Luisa, one of the few nurses able to speak English. There, they had become close, forging a friendship that would prove lifelong.

'She was critical of the regime,' an old friend, Katerina Diaz, told Slim via a video call from her home in Brazil. 'She was always outspoken, mostly about the conditions in the hospital and the local community, but after she retired from her work she started to criticise the government. She used to write political articles in Esperanto, which she learnt while she was nursing, then have them smuggled out of the country to be published overseas. It was inevitable someone would eventually come after her.'

'Did you know she planned to leave?'

'The last time I spoke to her was a year before she left. She told me she was thinking about going overseas for a while, that she had contacts. She told me nothing else, and when she finally left, her family contacted me. There was nothing I could tell them.' The old woman, easily ninety, smiled. 'And then I saw one of her pseudonyms in a magazine, and knew that wherever she was, she was still the old Maria-Luisa.'

'Thank you for talking to me.'

'Anytime.'

Slim ended the call and took a deep breath. He stared at the computer screen, still struggling to believe Chris had managed to find a living workmate of Maria-Luisa's who was willing—and able—to talk to him.

'Lots of copied emails,' Chris had told him with a grin. 'I was trying to avoid revising for my history exam.'

The call had explained a lot. Why Bob had come to be writing his thoughts in Esperanto, hiding them for everyone but himself, a private man keeping his thoughts close. It was extreme, but his Armed Forces days had left scars deeper than skin deep. Slim turned to a psychiatric assessment of Bob that Don had pulled some strings to find, and read again the passage that had struck him the hardest:

"Robert Harker is a deeply troubled individual. This paranoia manifests itself in acts of extreme self-destructive behaviour, which perhaps explains why he spent several years homeless. That he was able to recover can be attributed to exchanging one type of obsession—that of self-sabotage—for another, that of his current hobby, the creation of puppets and the writing of stage plays. That he has managed to channel his nervous energy into something creative is a quite remarkable turnaround. What remains concerning however is the possibility that unexpected external triggers might result in a reversion to his old behaviours."

Slim had fought off his own trauma using the bottle. That Bob had turned his heart and mind to the creative arts was impressive.

The pieces were starting to come together. The elephant in the room remained, though.

Where was Bob Harker?

Bob, a man haunted by his experiences in the Falklands War, had turned his mind to puppetry and scriptwriting. He had got his life back on track, only for an old friend to reappear, needing help. Bob had taken Maria-Luisa in, hidden her when her visa expired, and then nursed her when cancer took over her body. Afraid of the authorities, he had kept her hidden even after her death. For two weeks she had lain in his upstairs bedroom, dead, while Bob looked for a way to dispose of her body.

Had that been what he was doing out on the North Pier that day? Had he been planning to take her out there, give her over to the currents of the Bristol Channel?

The more that Slim thought about it, the more he felt certain that he was right. Bob, struggling with his emotions and the new trauma of dealing with his friend's body, had been seeking an extreme answer.

He had gone out onto the pier, and something had happened to him.

What?

Slim gripped the sides of his head, squeezing tight, trying to find a path through his muddled thoughts to the answer. Bob had gone out on to the pier, then the guard had lost sight of him in the mist. Had he ever made it to the end?

He was so close, but so much still made no sense.

Reggie had seen Bob's body, which had disappeared. And how was Bob appearing on the CCTV cameras at both Bristol and Portsmouth?

Unless of course...

...it wasn't Bob at all.

Slim packed up his laptop and headed out.

Richard Hardberry had confirmed the man was Bob, but a seed of doubt had been sown in Slim's mind. He headed straight for the Grand Pier. It had been a while since he had bumped into Reggie, but perhaps the man who had started this whole investigation could be of further use. When he reached the pier though, the sight of police tape outside Reggie's residential care home sent a cold chill down Slim's back, and as he saw a body bag being carried out of the building and into a waiting police van, he had no doubt in his mind who was inside.

48

'WHAT HAVE YOU STARTED, SLIM?' Karen, standing beside him by the pier rail that looked out to sea, shook her head. 'I'm getting out of my depth here.'

'How did he die?'

'He took his own life is what they're saying. He picked the lock on his door and hung himself over the stairs with a bedsheet tied around a banister.'

'Who found him?'

'One of the nurses.'

'Male or female?'

'What does that matter?'

'It just does.'

Karen sighed, pulled out a notebook and flipped through the pages.

'Male. Jonathan Long. Thirty-five, lives locally.'

'Run a background check on him. And get me the CCTV camera footage.'

'There was none in that part of the corridor.'

Slim gave a grim smile. 'Makes sense. Get forensics in there. It's murder until proven otherwise.'

'How do you know? There's no evidence——'

'There's Reggie. There's the way he looked at me. There are the eyes of a man who had already gone through everything——'

'And had had enough, by the look of things. There was a note——'

'I need to see it, or at least have a copy. This nurse, don't bring him in yet, but put a tail on him.'

'We don't have the resources for that.'

Slim clenched a fist, but said nothing. He let out a slow breath.

'Did you pick up James Jackson?'

'Yeah. He's in custody, charged with arson. He's looking at some serious time.'

'If I can prove it was coercion, what then?'

'Can you? What do you know that you're not telling me? You spoke to him, didn't you? What did he say? Slim, I offered to help you, but you have to help me. I'm struggling here.'

Slim said nothing. 'I can't find Bob,' he said. 'That's all I can tell you right now.'

Karen looked at him. 'You're infuriating.'

He smiled. His heart seemed to judder, and for once, he found the words he really wanted to say jumbling themselves into the correct order. 'In a few months, when this is over, can I buy you a coffee?'

'I'd like that,' she said. 'As long as it's strong.'

'Brewed yesterday,' Slim said. 'The best way.'

'Can you untangle this mess, Slim?'

He sighed and shrugged. 'I don't know. Maybe if I cut enough threads, I can at least have a good try.'

❧

'SLIM. You're still alive? I look for your obituary on a daily basis, wondering if I can claim my unpaid bills off your estate. No luck yet, I take it.'

'I'm on the cusp of riches, Alan,' Slim said with a smile. 'But until then, I could do with a sub.'

On the other end of the phone line, Alan Coaker, an old Armed Forces colleague of Slim's, coughed. 'There's a surprise. And I guess you want it yesterday.'

'You know me too well.'

'All right, tell me what you want, and I expect a dedication in your next book.'

'I knew I could rely on you, Alan.'

~

'HOW WAS YOUR FINAL EXAM?'

Chris shrugged. 'I'll find out in a couple of months. Feels good to get them over with.'

'Have you applied for Sixth Form yet?'

'Dunno. Not sure.'

'You should. Get your education while you can. Otherwise you'll forever be playing catch up.'

Chris rolled his eyes. 'You sound like … one of my teachers.'

'All I can teach you is how life will screw you up if you're not careful.'

'I know enough about that already.'

'How's your granddad?'

'Keeping his hands to himself for now. A police officer came round a couple of days ago. PC Tasker. Just said she was checking in. She asked about you. I'd swear she was blushing.'

Slim smiled. 'Good.'

Chris spread his hands. 'Right. So what's my next job? That's why you're bribing me with hamburgers, right?'

Slim looked down at Chris's empty plate. 'You need to put some meat on your bones,' he said. 'But since you asked, yes. I need you to follow someone. It could be something, could be nothing. Don't get close enough to be seen, and don't engage the person under any circumstances.'

'All right....'

Slim took a box out of his bag and slid it across the table. Coaker had come through, for once avoiding any of his little in-jokes.

'In here is a camera. If this guy leaves his house, makes a phone call, meets anyone, I want it recorded. Be subtle. Act like a tourist, like you're lost, whatever you need to do. And remember, don't get close; don't engage.'

Chris opened the box and pulled out a little object squeezed in beside the camera.

'What's this?'

'Police-issue taser. In case you get in any trouble.'

'Whoa. Huh, and there's a phone in here too.'

'It's a burner. It's only got one number on it—mine. If you need me or you see something suspicious, call me anytime.'

'Got it. Is this guy dangerous?'

'He might be. I don't know. Can you handle it?'

Chris shrugged. 'Maybe.' He leaned into the box again. 'Why are there some books in here?'

'In case you get bored. Surveillance is about as dull as a task can get.'

'Great. You're gonna pay me, right?'

Slim smiled. 'I hope so.'

49

SLIM STOOD BACK in the alleyway and watched the little motorboat pulling out from the harbour. It headed out into the bay, then made an abrupt turn to the north, heading straight into the mist that swirled further out in the Bristol Channel. Slim waited for a moment then walked back to where he had left his car. A few minutes later he pulled in at the lookout spot car park. A couple of men stood with cameras angled towards the North Pier, but with the mist cutting it off halfway there was little to see.

Slim looked around for the man he had spoken to before, but couldn't see him. Instead, he wandered up to a different man, an elderly gentleman who looked like the stoop he needed to peer into the lens was his natural posture, then cleared his throat.

'How's the pier today?'

The man looked up and smiled. 'The old girl's hanging in there.'

'Do you come up here often?'

'Every day. I'm working on a picture book. A year in

the life of a historical relic.' He laughed. 'I'm talking about the pier, not myself.'

Slim offered him a smile. 'Does much happen out there? No one sneaking out for a look, coming in on boats?'

'It's not about the people, is it? It's about the old girl herself, and how she stands there in all weather. I got some magnificent shots during that storm we had in March, even though I almost lost my camera. I mean, my pictures are of the pier, but I'll let the odd boat stay in there, just for perspective.'

'I'd love to see them, if you had time.'

The man's face lit up. 'A fellow enthusiast? I could just tell. Do you have an email? I have so many, I keep them in cloud storage online. I have a filtered file with ones that I might use for the book.'

'That would be great.' Slim gave the man his email and thanked him again. 'I see the mist is rolling in again,' he said.

The old man grinned. 'Magnificent, isn't it?'

Slim feigned enthusiasm for a few more minutes, then made his excuses and left. He drove slowly along the coast road, but the mist was so thick now he could barely see beyond the shoreline to the water. Frustrated, he headed back into the town.

The mist quickly turned to rain. Slim called Chris for an update, but Chris was holed up in a café and had nothing to report. He complimented Slim on his choice of paperbacks though.

'Top of the pile in the charity shop,' he said with a shrug. 'I didn't even read the titles.'

He went back to the B&B and found the old photographer had already sent him a link to an online file-sharing site where he stored his pictures of the pier. Slim started looking through a folder labelled BEST but even that had over two thousand photographs, the vast majority of which at first glance seemed to show the same thing. Slim looked through a few dozen but found himself getting restless, so he headed back out to the promenade and walked down to the Grand Pier.

It was after school had closed for the day, so the pier was filled with noisy kids playing video games or wandering aimlessly about to keep out of the rain. Slim went up to the theatre, ignored a CLOSED sign and went through the unlocked door. Fiona was sitting behind the reception desk, half-heartedly sorting piles of fliers while checking a smartphone lying nearby. She smiled as she noticed him.

'You can't keep away, can you?'

'The lure of the theatre. How is it today?'

'Grand opening next week. There's literal smoke coming out of Amanda's ears. Marius is fretting too, mostly because spring season was a washout and the rent's going up in July.'

'I'll grab a couple of tickets if it'll help out.'

'Ooh. Hot date?'

Slim shrugged. 'I like to stretch out.'

'Have you found Bob Harker yet?'

'Not even close. Could you do me a favour? I need another opinion on some CCTV footage.'

He took his laptop out of his bag and set it up on the reception desk. He played Fiona a composite of the two brief clips of Bob, watching for her reaction.

'This is him?' she said after a second watch through.

'Supposedly.'

'It looks like him. So he didn't die? He's gone on the run?'

'That's what the police think.'

'But it's not what you think?'

'I don't know what to think. Did you hear about Reggie Bowles?'

'I read it in the paper. I didn't know him well at all, but I saw him around from time to time. It just seems sad, don't you think?'

'Very. He had demons, did Reggie.'

'I can't imagine what would drive a man to do something like that.'

'Few of us can.'

Slim put away his laptop and slipped it back into his bag. He was about to leave when he looked up at the poster of the upcoming production and remembered something.

'I don't suppose … there's a young man here working on the production who lodged at Bob Harker's place a few years back. If I hunt out his name, do you think I could have a word? I'd just like to ask him about his impression of Bob. I'm clutching at straws at this point, but you never know. He might have something useful to say.'

'Sure.'

Slim gave Fiona the man's name and she went into the theatre, leaving him alone for a few minutes. He picked up a flyer for the upcoming show and was glancing at some still pictures on the back when she came back out.

'Sorry,' she said. 'He's been off the last few days with flu. I think I've got your number, haven't I? I can pass it on, get him to call you.'

'Thanks, that would be great.'

Fiona nodded and gave him a weary smile.

'Are you all right?'

She nodded. 'Ms. Smart doesn't like being interrupted.' Fiona made quotation marks in the air with her fingers. 'Not at "this critical moment".'

'Sorry about that.'

Fiona sighed. 'Don't worry, in a few weeks their special will have been filmed and the whole sorry lot of them will be off in some major London theatre, leaving us to get back to the sea shanties.'

'Hang in there,' Slim said.

She told him to take the leaflet, so he stuffed it into his pocket and headed back outside. The rain was pouring now, so he hurried up the pier, grabbed fish and chips from Richard Hardberry's stall and took them back to his B&B. There, he made some coffee from a machine in the lounge room downstairs and sat down at a window table to look over his notes.

Karen had called, pressing him for updates, but giving her incomplete or speculative information would help no one. And what few cards he had left to play he wanted to keep close to his chest.

On his list of things to do he found a number that had left a message a couple of days ago that he was yet to call back. He made the call, listening to the smooth, radio-friendly drawl on the other end.

'Is this John Hardy? The private investigator? Thanks for your call back.'

'Is this Nathan English?'

'You got me. Say, would you be interested in coming on the show some time? My listeners would love it.'

'There's not much of interest that I could tell them,' Slim said, uncomfortable at the very thought. 'Sorry I didn't get back to you sooner. I'm in the middle of an investigation.'

'Wow, live from the crime scene.'

'I wouldn't say that. I wanted to ask about a guest you had on your podcast show a while back. Larry Amiss?

Formerly a member of the so-called E-boys, a local gang active in the nineties?'

'Ah, yes, I remember. What can I help you with?'

'He talked about a man called Jackie Ackerman, who died in a stabbing in the mid-nineties. I just wondered what else he might have said, off the record.'

'Wow, that's going back a bit. I can dig out my notes. We did have a chat before going on air, but I can't really remember. Can I ask why you're interested?'

'The man who killed Ackerman, Frederick "Reggie" Bowles, was involved in my current investigation.'

'Was?'

Slim scowled inwardly, annoyed at the slip. He should have realised that someone whose job was interviewing people would pick up on every word.

'He died a couple of days ago. He took his own life.'

Nathan English whistled. 'Phew. Your investigation is ongoing, I take it? Perhaps if you came on the show, you could spread a little public awareness.'

'All I really want to know is why Reggie killed Ackerman.'

'Okay. I'll hunt out my notes. All I remember specifically that Larry Amiss said off the record was that some guys in that business struggled to leave it behind.'

'The gang is still active?'

'Maybe not under the same name, but yeah. He said gangs, like most industries, evolve over time.'

50

HE RECEIVED another email from Kay. No news on the DNA sample from Bob's ring, but he had worked through some more of the charred puppet remains. Hidden inside one he found an empty pill bottle. Fragments of translations that Kay had recovered included phrases such as "I never thought the tunnel would end, but after all these years I can see light again", and "when I look at the faces of the smiling children I can believe for a moment that I might have been forgiven."

'He's talking about overcoming his trauma,' Kay wrote in the email. 'My guess is that this character was The Doctor. The empty pill bottle shows that Bob no longer needs treatment, and some of the expressions suggest he's managed to overcome his problems.'

There was more. The most extensive remains were for a puppet Kay guessed was The Minstrel.

'The translated fragments seem to tell a story,' Kay told Slim later over the phone. 'Something about a shipwreck, and trying to find salvation. Most of it's lost, of course. In the middle of the puppet I found what seems to be the pieces of a flute.'

'That's great, Kay.'

'Do you have any idea what it means?'

Slim shook his head. 'No idea. But some kind of therapy sounds like a possibility.'

'That's what it looks like, for sure. My guess is that it fuelled his creativity, that the shows he performed were an extension of his feelings. It sounds like he was an interesting man. You don't have any video footage of him, do you?'

'I don't.'

'A shame. I imagine his shows were eye-opening. I can't guess at what he was thinking, but there might have been a clue as to what happened to him.'

Slim gave Chris a call and asked him if he could contact the families of the people who had identified Bob. There was a narrow chance. Chris, holed up in the same café near to the house of the man he was following, jumped at the chance.

Slim packed his things and headed downstairs, only to be met by the landlady in the entrance.

'Mr Hardy? A letter arrived for you this morning.'

He thanked her and took the letter, trying to remember who he might have given his address to. Opening it, he smiled at the private note from Fiona, addressed as "from one sleuth to another". She explained that she had spotted his car while walking her dog and guessed his location. Inside the envelope were two complimentary tickets to the opening performance of the stage show, "just in case no one shows up".

Slim smiled and put the letter into his bag.

Slightly alarmed at how easy he had been to find, he moved his car a little further away and then walked back into the town. He was nearly at the pier when he got a call from Karen.

'He's shown up again,' she said.

'Bob?'

'Yesterday. We've got a few seconds of grainy CCTV footage from Victoria Coach Station in London. He can be seen limping out of the main entrance and away in the direction of Eccleston Square. He goes out of shot, then that's it.'

'Do you know what bus he arrived on?'

'One from Portsmouth arrived just ten minutes before the time stamp on the video footage, so we're working on getting a passenger manifest, but so far we're having no luck. We've already interviewed the driver, but he said no one matching Bob's description was on board.'

'It's a deliberate ruse. We need more footage. We also need passenger manifests for all the buses that came in that morning. We need to speak to everyone we can.'

'It could take months, Slim.'

'Can you get me concourse footage from ten minutes before Bob was seen, from Victoria, Portsmouth and also Bristol? Any camera angle is fine, and it doesn't matter whether it shows Bob or not.'

'I can probably get it but we've been through it already. There was no sign of Bob.'

'If you can, just email me the files. I want to take another look.'

There was a pause. 'All right. If you think you know something, please tell me, Slim.'

'All I know right now is where Bob Harker isn't. And that … might be important.'

51

SITTING in a rainy café while waiting for Karen's email, he trawled through the photo gallery of the North Pier the old photographer had sent him. To his untrained eye the pictures seemed to change little except for the weather, with a few gorgeous shots of the pier's island emerging from thick fog to others of the pier set against glorious sunsets. There were a couple of it dusted with snow and some with the old pier being battered by vicious storm waves.

All of which would make a lovely picture book, but were of no use to Slim whatsoever.

Also with the file marked "best", there was another labelled "outtakes". Slim opened it, then gulped at the list of nearly twenty thousand files. Fearing for his eyes, he began to flick through them.

Many were awkward angles, close-ups, long range, obstructions in view. Dozens featured vehicles moving past at exactly the wrong moment, corners of buildings or cars that needed trimming. Slim smiled at the blurred seabird wing that took up half of one photo. Fearing for his eyes, he took a break to order another coffee, then got back down to work.

Many of them looked like good photos to Slim, but had ships passing in the background, large car transporters or barges, too close or too far away for a pleasing aesthetic. Fishing boats too, were numerous, passing behind the island, none pretty enough to look good in a picture book.

Patterns, he reminded himself. *I'm looking for patterns.*

And then, just when the monotony was about to make his head explode, he saw it.

A little green fishing boat, coming in close to the island, dropping anchor. Always in thick fog, few shots showed more than part of the boat at a time, but if composited, there would be enough to make a clear picture.

And there, on the same day, a man leaning into the window of the security van.

Slim flicked forward, eyes aching as the pictures blurred. A month passed. There was the boat again, just a triangle of green visible in the fog. The off-cut photo showing a corner of the van, a uniformed man opening a bolted gate that led out into a white void.

He needed to speak to Karen. This was big. If this was as big as he suspected it was, he couldn't deal with this alone.

He reached into his bag for his phone, but as he pulled it out, it buzzed in his hand. He dropped it on the floor, then scrabbled like an idiot for it, scooping the battered old Nokia up before the caller could ring off.

'Kay?'

'Slim? The DNA results came back. Jesus, Slim, you need to see this. This is big.'

'That sample matched with someone? From the Falklands War?'

'You've got bigger problems than that,' Kay said. 'It

matched with a dead man who washed up on a beach further up the Bristol Channel in late 1996. I found the file online. Joshua Cately. He had been a known homeless man in the Bristol area. An addict. He was found on a beach near Clevedon by a dog walker, and a murder case was opened. It went cold not long after, with no evidence to make a case.'

'He drowned?'

'His neck was broken and what was left of his face showed signs of a severe beating. He was dead before he hit the water.'

52

JOSHUA CATELY. Donald Lane was able to pull more from the internet than Slim could find, but the man had been a fleeting moment, born of addict parents, graduating from a hellish childhood to a full-time life on the streets. Just twenty-one when he died, a young man who had slipped into one of life's cracks and not had the strength to claw his way back out.

A man found dead on a beach, the bag sewn shut, the case closed.

And now his DNA was on the military signet ring Bob Harker had buried in the centre of a papier-mâché puppet labelled the Devil, wrapped in shreds of unreadable text which translated into something of a confession.

Cately had been homeless prior to his death. It was likely Bob Harker had also been homeless during the same period.

Slim looked at a map which showed the sea currents along the Bristol Channel. His conclusion didn't require much of a leap of faith.

What Reggie had said about fighting for his life, it

carried so much more meaning now. Reggie and Bob had shared more than just walks on the beach. They had carried a collective darkness with them, one which Slim had to uncover.

Homeless men didn't go out onto an abandoned pier to fight for no reason.

Slim found Kay's notes, the meaning of Bob's hidden words far clearer now.

We had no choice. It was me or him, or both of us. And I knew how, and he didn't. Me or him. Why was I there? I had no choice. He had no choice either. We fought to win, to survive.

The devil rides with me. Every step. He sits there, and he goads me, and he tells me what I did wrong. And sometimes he shows me that man's face, and all the pieces that I've glued together start to come apart.

I knew how. He didn't. And the cheers as he fell made my heart and soul cry.

The cheers. Other people had been there. Bob and Joshua, vulnerable homeless men, had been forced to fight for the entertainment of others out on the North Pier, where no one would hear their cries, no one would hear their screams.

Reggie had been one of them too, and perhaps there had been others.

Slim searched online. He found rumours, speculation. No one had ever been prosecuted, even questioned. Perhaps Joshua Cately's death had brought an end to things, sent the perpetrators into hiding.

His mind reeling with the impact of this new information, Slim headed outside, down onto the beach where the wind had got up, whipping sand across his face as he walked out to the low tide mark, to where the sand began to suck at his boots, the water to rush in towards him, filling in his footprints as he walked along the water's edge.

Even when a couple of bigger waves caught him, the water soaking his boots and socks, he continued to walk until eventually he came to the far end of the beach, where the little boat that belonged to Robert Tiller lay on sand exposed by the retreated tide, lying among a flotilla of other marooned boats.

And he remembered the words James Jackson had traced out on the dashboard of Slim's car with one shaking finger, so hard to follow that had James not whispered the words at the same time Slim might not have understood.

I don't know his name but he came to our school.

53

I WISH the water had swallowed me.

And it nearly had. Among the medical records for Bob Harker that Donald Lane had pulled from the internet was an early one dated June 1996, when Bob had been found near the rocks at the northern end of Sandy Bay Beach, barely a mile along the Bristol Channel from the old pier, soaking wet and suffering from hypothermia. Rushed to hospital, he had been treated for the effects of near-drowning, and in an attached police incident report, Bob claimed to have got in trouble during an early morning swim. However, he was fully clothed, and had the appearance of having been in the water for some considerable time. Bob's hands and face showed signs of abrasive damage, which he claimed had been due to trying to drag himself out of the sea onto the rocks during a heavy swell.

With little other explanation to go on, a note had been added declaring Bob not of sound mind, recommending his admittance to a psychiatric hospital once his physical condition had improved.

As far as Slim could tell, the event marked the end of

Bob's life on the streets. He had been incarcerated for a while, then been considered well enough for council housing in 2001. He had lived alone ever since, claiming benefits while making a little side money working as a Punch and Judy performer, then later renting out a spare room to students from Bristol.

Three weeks after Bob had been admitted to hospital, Joshua Cately's remains had been found on a beach further up the Bristol Channel.

The two events had never been connected.

From a viewing spot overlooking Robert Tiller's sailing club, Slim called Nathan English.

'This is John Hardy. Any luck with finding your notes on Larry Amiss?'

'Not yet. I remembered something he said about Ackerman, though. He told me Ackerman liked to goad people, put the fear of God in them. I cut that section out of the interview because it was rambling, but I remember him saying that Ackerman was a bully, that he got off on tormenting people. He said it was likely the man who'd stabbed him had snapped. Ackerman was either known to him or had hurt him in some way.'

'Thanks.'

'I'll hunt out the original recording and send you a copy.'

'I appreciate your help.'

Slim hung up. Out to sea, the mist had begun to roll in. He sat down on a wall, stuffed his hands into his pockets and waited.

Robert Tiller's car pulled into the sailing club's car park a few minutes later. Slim watched as the man, dressed in a suit and sunglasses, got out and went inside. A few minutes later he reappeared, dressed in fishing gear and a life jacket, and climbed into his boat. As the fog rolled in,

Tiller started his engine and headed up around the headland.

It was time to bring the man in. Slim pulled out his phone to call Karen, but as he did so, it buzzed with an incoming call.

It took him a moment to recognise the unidentified number as that of the burner phone he had given to Chris.

'Slim? That guy you've got me following, he took a bus up to the old pier. I followed him. There's no one around, but it looks like—'

'Stay there, Chris! Keep off—'

The phone went dead. Slim looked down, cursing himself for not charging his phone battery. With a grunt of frustration, he pushed it into his pocket and stood up.

Down by the water, Tiller's boat was nowhere to be seen. And where the Bristol Channel had been, there was now just a wall of impenetrable mist.

54

The narrow, twisting lanes weren't conducive for driving at speed, but Slim pressed the pedal where he could, endured a couple of frustrated honks from other drivers and finally pulled into the car park near the North Pier ten minutes later. Below him, the world appeared to end where the road arced around the rocky shoreline.

The old photographer he had seen before was packing his equipment away into the back of his car. Slim rushed over, startling the man, who let out a gasp of fright.

'Did you see anyone go onto the pier?' Slim asked.

'No, no, you can't see anything now. My day's done, I'm afraid.'

'I have to go out there. I need you to call the police for me. Ask for PC Karen Tasker. Tell her Slim Hardy called. Coastguard and police to the North Pier.'

'What's going on?'

'Call her, please.'

Slim didn't wait to see if the man made the call or not. He ran down a set of steps from the car park, crossed the road, and leapt at the steel fence blocking the entrance to the old pier. He was halfway over when a shout came from behind him.

The security van had been parked a little way up the street, out of view. Now a burly man came running down the road, hollering at Slim to get down.

Slim remembered the pictures he had seen, of a man leaning into the window of the security van. A man who wore Robert Tiller's suit. As the security guard reached him, Slim picked his moment, then aimed a vicious kick with his boot, twisting his foot at the last moment to avoid the man's grasping hands. It gave a satisfying crunch as it connected with the man's nose, then the security guard was staggering backwards, blood dripping through his fingers as he cursed and swore at Slim.

Slim was over the fence in a moment. When he reached the walkway that crossed the old pier he glanced back, worried the security guard would be after him, but the man was staggering back up the road towards his van, clutching his face.

The man would return, or he would call someone, and neither of them were options that would help Slim. The pier slowly unfolded in front of him as Slim ran into the mist. At one point halfway, he doubled over, gasping for breath, and looked up to find that neither the land nor the island were visible, as though he stood in the middle of some kind of purgatorial bridge. For a moment disoriented as to which way was back and which forward, he looked down at the sea through the cracks in the boards below him, saw a rising swell rolling in to crash against the rocks protruding from the sea, and picked his spot.

The island appeared out of the swirling white, the clock tower in front of him, the ruined building of the old lifeboat station to his left, the rest of the island behind. He reached the corner of the old lifeboat building and peered round. The ruined main building stood in front of him, the mist hiding the sea behind. Slim saw no one, so crept forward. He was halfway across the cracked, weed-strewn concrete when he heard voices.

'You did well.'

'I need money to get out of the country before they catch up with me.'

'You made it look like a suicide.'

'Even so—'

'Don't worry.'

Slim crept closer to the main building. Part of its roof had caved in, guttering hung broken, and hardy creepers had begun to devour one corner, but it was still intact enough to provide shelter. The voices came from inside. He dropped down by a hole where a window had been and risked a glance into the gloomy interior.

Two men stood inside, under the only part of the roof still standing. Robert Tiller had his hands in his pockets. The other man, Jonathan Long, the nurse from Reggie's residential care home, stood with his hand on the wall nearby.

'What if he talked? He wouldn't stop going on the last few days. About Ackerman. About what you made him do out here. About the guys that died—'

'He's talking rubbish. He doesn't know anything.'

'What if it comes back on me? I've got to get out of the country.'

Tiller walked over, moving slowly, casually. 'Look, don't worry. Bowles was a no one. He won't be missed. In a couple of weeks no one will remember he was ever here.'

'They'll figure it out and it'll come back on me—'

Tiller moved with astonishing speed. He closed the distance between them in an instant, one hand slipping free, something glinting in his hand for a moment before it entered the softness of Jonathan Long's stomach with a smooth squelching sound. Long gasped, Tiller twisted the knife, and Long tried to push him back, but his strength had gone. He pressed uselessly at Tiller's shoulders, like a dance partner indicating a new move. Robert growled, pushing him back against the wall, then pulled the knife free and stepped back, letting Long slump over forward and crash to the ground.

'You should have kept your mouth shut,' Tiller said, watching Long, who continued to twitch for a few seconds and then exhaled one last breath before falling still. 'Nothing ever works as well as silence.'

A sharp snap came from the other side of the building. Tiller turned, tossed the knife on the ground, then headed for the old entranceway. Slim, a terrible sinking feeling in his stomach, starting moving too, back along the wall, mirroring Robert's movements, his heart breaking in advance as he saw Chris's gangly, awkward shape break from the shadows and run hard for the walkway.

Tiller paused a moment, pulled something hard and metallic from his pocket, lifted it, took aim.

'Robert, no!'

Tiller flinched slightly at Slim's cry. The gun went off. Chris jerked, arms flailing, then hit the ground hard, rolling sideways as Tiller turned the gun on Slim.

'Hardy? What the hell? You followed me here? You and your friend?'

'He's nothing to do with this!'

'Nothing to do with what? Nothing happened here. I can make three bodies vanish as well as one. The currents here … they're unforgiving.'

As though to emphasise his point, the wind gave a sudden howl and a heavy wave cracked against the island's rear retaining wall.

Beyond Tiller's shoulder, Chris was twitching, one arm scrabbling at the ground as though he were trying to get up. Slim tried to hold Tiller's attention, aware that Chris was a sitting duck.

'The best wolf is the one who hunts in plain sight. Isn't that right, Robert? All that activism, just a cover. The school visits, just a way to recruit. Like you did with James Jackson, the kid you paid to torch Bob Harker's place.'

Tiller lifted an eyebrow. 'Is that what you think?'

Tiller took a step closer. Less than twenty paces separated them; nothing for a man with decent aim. Slim was desperate to get to Chris, but while alive he could help the boy, dead he was worthless to anyone. Chris was still moving, but from his groans it was clear he was badly hurt.

Distract him. Keep him talking. And hope.

'Harker was involved in those homeless fights you organised out here back in the nineties. Why? Gambling, I suppose. Of course it was. Harker killed someone, beat them to death. You got scared, knew if he talked your whole operation would be shut down. The gambling, the drugs—'

'What are you talking about?'

'When's your next shipment due, Robert? I've seen your little green boat. The police are looking for it right now. You're going away whether you shoot me or not.'

'You're a liar.'

'Am I? Harker killed a man, knew he was dead, so he jumped, didn't he? Into the sea. You thought he was dead until you saw his picture in the papers, and knew you could still be exposed.'

'You're out of your mind.'

From somewhere through the fog came a thick beating sound, like the thudding wings of a giant moth batting against a window.

'I have just one question,' Slim said. 'Where's Bob Harker? Do you know? Because I don't. And that's the only question I want answered. He came out here the day you were doing a pickup, didn't he? He got in your way.'

A police helicopter appeared out of the fog, hovering over the island. Tiller glanced up with a look of despair on his face, then tightened his grip on the gun.

'Here!'

The cry came from Chris, his arm swinging, something rattling across the stones. The taser, tossed as though Chris thought it worked like a grenade. It was nowhere near Slim, coming to a stop somewhere behind Robert, near a concrete step down to the walkway, but it was the distraction Slim needed as Robert looked away. He rushed forward, lowering his centre of balance, and barrelled into Robert Tiller's midriff. The gun went off close enough to make his ears ring, then Tiller was grappling with him, trying to get the gun into position. A fist struck Slim's face once, twice, three times, then Tiller knocked him away. Slim rolled, coming up into a sitting position to find Tiller crouched nearby, the gun raised. Then Tiller jerked, caught in an electric current, legs and arms kicking out.

As Tiller rolled sideways, an ashen face appeared, the taser clutched in one hand. Jonathan Long, shirt soaked with blood, shuffled closer to Tiller and shocked him again, then slumped forward onto his face. Slim looked at Chris, realised the throw had never been intended for him but for the injured man, and began crawling towards his young protégé, as behind him, the police helicopter landed.

55

SLIM'S INJURIES WERE SLIGHT, a few bruises, a dislocated jaw quickly reset. He paced the corridor outside the emergency ward while Chris was in surgery, hating himself, praying to a god he didn't believe in that Chris would be all right, all too aware that the boy had indirectly saved Slim's life while Slim had done nothing but put the boy in danger.

Never again. I will never put anyone in front of me again.

The nearest pub and its numbness beckoned him more strongly than it had in months, but whenever he felt on the verge of giving in, he looked around at the seats in the waiting room.

Chris's grandfather had been notified but hadn't come.

The doors opened and a doctor appeared. Slim tried not to look too desperate as he asked for an update.

The doctor smiled. 'He'll be fine. The bullet passed through the flesh of his shoulder. We had to do a little surgery and give him some blood, but as gunshot wounds go, it was minor. He was a lucky boy. Six inches to the right would have been a different story.'

'Thank you so much.'

The doctor nodded. 'He'll need an hour or two to wake up from the anaesthetic, then you can see him.'

Slim could only nod, then slump down onto a hard plastic chair, leaning his head against the wall, wrapped in the arms of a sense of relief that felt like the most comfortable armchair in the world.

He was still sitting that way some minutes later when Karen found him.

She sat down in the chair beside his, then handed him a coffee from the machine down the corridor.

'Where do we start?' she said.

'He could have died,' Slim said. 'As it is, he's scarred for life, and that's my fault. I thought I could help him. Instead, I almost got him killed. It's my fault. Everything.'

'I'll berate the living hell out of you for getting a kid involved in your operation later,' Karen said. 'But for now, he's alive, you're alive, and even more of a surprise, Jonathan Long survived his surgery too. That will be an interesting conversation, I can tell you.'

'He survived? Really?'

'Touch and go, but he's stable.'

'Tiller?'

'In custody. Keeping his mouth shut, but we have so much on him we could put him away for a hundred years. That green boat you spotted, we traced it to an Irish port. It was loaded up with illegal goods, everything from class A drugs to firearms. We're in the process of busting a major gang. You did your best to screw it up, but luckily your young assistant has a decent head on his shoulders. He recorded everything on his phone. Tiller's likely to be prosecuted for several cold case deaths we can link to that island.' She smiled and sighed as she looked at him. 'Out of the carnage, you did good, Slim. Somehow, you did good. People won't die because of the drugs now taken off the streets. A major operation has at least had its claws cut, and kids like James Jackson won't be groomed into a life of crime by Robert Tiller and his lies anymore.'

'How is James?'

'We have a recording of Tiller admitting to what he did. James is likely to get a slap on the wrist, but that's about it.'

'That's something. James is still young enough to make something of his life.'

'As are you.'

Slim couldn't help but laugh. 'I've made enough of it already,' he said.

～

It wasn't until the next day that Slim was allowed to visit Chris. He showed up with a bag of grapes and a handful of magazines he had bought at random from the newsagent in the hospital lobby.

Chris was sitting up in bed, his shoulder strapped up, an intravenous drip sticking out of his arm. He turned as Slim sat down and smiled.

'We busted him, didn't we?'

'You did. I nearly screwed it up.' Slim scratched his chin. 'You know, I've been going over what I should say to you. A lot of different things. How I regret getting you involved, how you never should have followed Long onto that old pier, how I thought you'd died ... but all I can really say is that you did good. You should never have been anywhere near that place, but ... you did good.' He smiled as Chris chuckled, then winced as his shoulder pulled. 'People's lives have been saved, and some bad people will get put away, and that's thanks to you being braver than any fifteen-year-old kid should be. But please don't do it again.'

Chris grinned again. 'I'm sixteen.'

Slim shrugged. 'I'm not good with ages. Or names, or dates.'

'Or charging your phone, so PC Tasker said.'

Slim pulled the battered old Nokia out of his pocket and turned it over in his hands. 'Top piece of machinery, this. Could survive a nuclear war. It's easy to forget to plug it in when it only needs charging once a year. Not like this modern rubbish you kids have.'

'I thought they were wind up?'

Slim smiled. 'That's the previous model.' His smile dropped. 'Has your granddad shown up yet?'

Chris shook his head. 'Not yet. No real surprise there. I'm glad you came, though.'

'I'll come every day until you get out of here. Then I'll take you for some ice cream or popcorn or whatever you kids eat.'

'Deal. Do you reckon we'll get a summer this year?'

Slim glanced at the window, which had a view of a gloomy grey sky. 'I doubt it. This is Britain after all.'

'Wouldn't feel right if we did, would it?'

Slim shook his head. 'It wouldn't.'

'Have you found Bob Harker yet?'

Slim sighed. 'Not yet.'

'Keep looking. You're close, I know it.'

'Maybe. Maybe not.'

The doctor arrived shortly after to administer some medicine, so Slim took his leave. As he was going out through the waiting room, he stopped in surprise at the sight of the group of youths standing in front of him.

Some of them from the park were there, a couple from

the kebab shop. At the front stood Ace, the same kid Slim had bashed with the table.

'What are you doing here?' Slim said.

Ace looked at his feet. 'We came to see C. To see Chris.'

'Why?'

The kid shrugged. 'He's a mate.'

'Is he?'

One of the others stepped forward. 'That guy who was arrested … he came to our school. My brother, he got him into dealing, taking stuff. He overdosed last September. Died. That guy was a scumbag.'

Slim looked from face to face. When Ace looked up, Slim extended a hand. 'Sorry I messed your face up,' he said. 'I was just jealous. I looked like hell even at your age.'

It took a moment for the kid to get the joke. Then he gave a thin smile and took Slim's hand. 'You're all right, man.'

'Are we good?'

'Yeah. We're good.'

Slim smiled. 'Stay off the booze and drugs. Stay out of prison. Pick up litter and help old dears across the street. You got all of that?'

There were a few chuckles among the group.

'Yeah, man,' Ace said. 'We'll do our best.'

'But coffee,' Slim said, 'coffee is good for you. Especially if it was brewed yesterday.'

~

He called Karen when he got outside. A light wind blew across the car park, ruffling his hair.

'Slim?'

'I've just spoken to Chris.'

'How is he?'

'No thanks to me, he's fine.'

'What happens next, Slim?'

He stuffed one hand in his pocket and felt a crumpled envelope there.

'I need a couple of days off. Do you fancy going to the theatre?'

56

THE THEATRE WAS NOT QUITE SOLD out, with Slim and Karen able to get seats near the centre, a few rows back from the stage. Karen had dressed up for it, but Slim had come in his regular clothes, much to her disapproval.

While he could appreciate the value of the production, he quickly tired of the performance itself, a metaphysical story about a man lost at sea, shipwrecked on a remote island. There, the break from the norm occurred, with the shipwrecked sailor turning mad from lack of food and clean water, and finding himself faced with a series of nightmarish entities, all of whom required some form of confession before the sailor could move on. Slim was just wondering whether to excuse himself for the toilet and then make a break for the restaurant outside when one of the actors said something that brought his attention right back.

'The devil rides with me. Every step.'

Slim frowned. As he recognised another line, he reached down for his bag and fiddled through it for his notes.

'What are you doing?' Karen hissed.

'I need to check something.'

'Right now?'

'Yes, right now.'

He pulled out the sheaf of printouts, took a torch from his pocket and began scanning them, ignoring the annoyed muttering from the seats behind.

He shone his light on one quote just as the actor spoke an almost identical line. He put the notes away, then leaned close to Karen.

'Did you bring your badge?'

'I always carry it with me.'

'Good. We need to make an arrest after the show.'

'Why?'

'I think I know who killed Bob Harker. And why.'

～

THE GIRL LOOKED TIRED as she came out of the changing room, a bag slung over her shoulder. Slim stood back, attempting to appear incognito as he let Karen do her police work. A couple of minutes later he found himself driving behind Karen's patrol car as they headed for the station.

He wanted to join the interview, but Karen made him wait outside. He paced the waiting area for a while, restless, too wired to even sit down. When Karen emerged from the interview less than half an hour later, he bounded over to her like an enthusiastic dog.

'You were right,' she said, giving him a begrudging smile. 'She confessed that she didn't write that script, but that it was given to her by her boyfriend, Sam.'

'Who lodged with Bob Harker, but was unceremoniously kicked out when Bob needed room for Maria-Luisa.

He stole some of Bob's papers, realised he had found a script for one of Bob's shows. Maybe Bob had been channelling his problems into art, into his performances, perhaps as a form of therapy. This student Sam read it, thought it was pretty good, and gave it to his girlfriend.'

'We've sent a car to pick him up, put his picture out to the transport police. We'll bring him in.'

'I want to talk to him.'

'This is police business now, Slim. You've done everything you could do. You should go back and rest for a while.'

'Karen—'

She put a hand on his chest, a little too tenderly perhaps, so she snatched it quickly away as though forgetting herself.

'Slim ... you have to let the police deal with this now. This is a murder investigation. I don't want to sound like I'm not grateful, but we both know you got lucky with Robert Tiller. I need this to go through the proper police channels.'

He must have looked crestfallen because this time when she reached up to put a hand on his chest, she let it linger there while she said, 'I'll call you, Slim. I'll need you, for sure. If not for this ... then for me.'

There was nothing more he could say. He walked from the police station down to the beach, where he paced the sands until sea mist turned to drizzle and forced him into a seafront café. There he sat brooding with his laptop open in front of him but the screen blank, staring out at the drizzling rain, the grey waves lapping at the distant shore.

Was it really over? Karen hadn't given him the full name of the former student who had lodged at Bob's place, but Slim had gone through Chris's list then compared it to what he had found online.

Samuel Richards. From Bristol, he had failed his final exams in 2017, retaking and passing a year later. Now he worked on costume design and make-up, with credits available online for a couple of minor stage shows in the Westcountry area.

Had he blamed Bob for failing his exams and then stolen his script as an act of revenge? But even if he had, was that reason enough to murder Bob several years later?

Make-up and costume design. It was something that had slipped past Slim as a job title, but now that he thought about it, was it significant?

Slim switched on his laptop and brought up the three CCTV videos that supposedly showed Bob in Bristol, Portsmouth and London. Bob's appearance lasted for no longer than a couple of seconds in each, but the videos themselves were several minutes long. Slim watched them through a couple of times, then closed his laptop and stood up.

There was still work to do.

57

Tim Fernby, the driver from the local bus company who had been one of the last people to see Bob alive, stared at the screen and frowned.

'Is that supposed to be him there?'

'Yes. The one with the overlarge backpack.'

Tim shook his head. 'No, that's not him. I mean, it's similar, but it's kind of exaggerated, if you know what I mean. His pack wasn't that big, and he didn't stoop quite like that. If you didn't see him that often you could think it, but I watched him walk away from the bus hundreds of times.'

'Are you sure?'

'Positive. Plus, Bob's limp was on the other leg. It wasn't as pronounced as that, either. You'd only really notice it if you saw him a lot.'

Slim nodded. 'Thanks for your help.'

He phoned Marius at the theatre and asked to talk to

Amanda Smart. After first displaying some of the ferocity Fiona had warned Slim about in berating him for ruining her stage play, she was able to check the log books and tell Slim that Samuel Owens had been off work sick on each of the days that Bob had appeared on CCTV. For the London date, he had been away for a day either side, citing a bout of flu.

Long enough to get to London, pick his spot and time, and get back again.

Looking again at the CCTV footage, he spotted a figure in two of the shots that closely resembled Samuel, one a minute before, the other a minute after. And he felt sure that if the police used some kind of facial recognition software or viewed a longer sample, they would find him somewhere in the crowd on the third.

Samuel Owens had deliberately impersonated Bob in order to set a trail leading the police away. Why else would he do so if he wasn't responsible for Bob's murder?

~

HE SENT what he had found to Karen, but he had to stew for a couple of days, waiting for her to reply. When he answered her phone call, however, what she had to say came as a surprise.

'He's admitted everything. Stealing the script, giving it to his girlfriend, then later impersonating Bob to make us think he was on the run over Maria-Luisa's death. He said he was bitter about being kicked out of Bob's place at short notice. It disrupted his study, and he lost a postgraduate opportunity as a result. We've searched his flat and found the costume he used to impersonate Bob.' Karen chuckled. 'It's pretty ingenious. The backpack part is inflatable. The kid's got some talent, that's for sure. Even if this could see him blacklisted for a while.'

'What about Bob? Did Samuel Owens kill him?'

'He denies it and we've found no evidence. He has an airtight alibi for the day Bob disappeared. He was in France with his girlfriend. We have details of his travel, passport stamps, the lot. And there are no forensics.'

'Why put on the show of impersonating Bob?'

'He said he got scared when he heard Bob had vanished and later that he might have killed someone. He decided to pretend Bob was still alive to keep us from looking too closely at Bob's life. He didn't want his girlfriend being busted for the stolen manuscript. He said he knew it was stupid after the first time, but he'd dug himself a hole and had no choice but to keep trying to cover it up.'

'And you believe him?'

'I believe the evidence, and the evidence believes him.'

'So … we still don't know what happened to Bob?'

Karen sighed. 'Unless you have anything you're not telling me?'

'Nope. I'm out.'

'Then I suppose the case is still open.'

Slim was too despondent to reply.

❧

BAD WEATHER CAME hard for the next couple of days, keeping Slim inside the B&B. He had talked to Karen about continuing the case, but with Robert Tiller in custody the police had their breakthrough. Jonathan Long had begun to talk in return for a plea deal and police protection. He had spoken at length about how he had been ordered by Tiller to silence Reggie Bowles after Reggie had begun to go on about fighting on the pier and killing Jackie Ackerman after recognising Jackie on the street one day when Jackie had mocked him. Tiller had feared what else Reggie's sporadic memory might have recalled, but when Chris had trailed Long to the old pier, their plan had backfired.

Emails were starting to come in, other cases that yearned for Slim's attention. He had earned nothing from the Bob Harker investigation, several weeks in various B&Bs had depleted his meagre savings, and his book royalties were running out. One or two of the cases were offering the kind of money that was hard to refuse for a man who worked from one payday to another.

In Weston, the summer was starting to show its face. Chris had been released from hospital and with Slim's help had found himself a short-term let. Slim had been unable to offer much advice on cooking or general housekeeping, but Karen had offered to stop by from time to time. Chris was hoping it was only temporary anyway, having applied to a Sixth Form college for September. With Karen able to back him up, plus the likelihood of a local medal for bravery on the horizon, he would have little difficulty getting a place, even if his exam results were worse than he hoped.

Slim called Karen to inform her that he planned to head inland to work on a new case. She picked him up and they went for a drive out to the North Pier.

'What happened to the guards?' Slim asked, noting the absence of a van by the security fence.

'Two of them admitted to taking bribes to turn a blind eye to what was going on at the other end of the pier,' she said. 'J&L Development Ltd are looking for another security company.'

'I'd like to take another look around out there, if you think it would be possible,' Slim said.

'I'm a police officer,' Karen said with a smile. 'Of course it's possible.'

They walked out along the old pier to the island. The tide was out, shingle visible below them, crusted with barnacles and dried seaweed. From here, following the curve of the shore, you could walk right back to the beach below the Grand Pier without ever going near the road. Slim paused for a moment, wondering.

He came to a stop in front of the old clock tower with the missing face, then pointed at a heap of rusting metal poles lying nearby.

'I wondered about those when I was out here the other day,' he said, going to the nearest and pulling a length of metal pole out of the pile. 'It's scaffolding. It must have surrounded the old clock tower, but collapsed.'

He had broken into the base of the tower before, finding only gloom and dirt, but now his mind started to race. He hadn't looked inside, hadn't seen what might be jammed higher up.

'Help me,' he said to Karen, going back to the hole he had made and pulling the rocks free once more.

'You don't really think he's in there, do you?'

'I don't know. I just want to look.'

Together, they broke away enough of the rocks to make a crawl space big enough to squeeze inside. With Karen begging him to be careful, Slim took a torch and shimmied in on his back, until he could look up the shaft of the tower at the debris lodged inside.

'What if he came out here for some reason, then encountered Robert Tiller doing a drug deal?' he muttered aloud, as much to himself as to Karen. 'They couldn't have thrown him in the sea because it was low tide. I checked. And if the mist had cleared, they'd be in full view of those photographers up on the viewing point. They had to hide his body somewhere quickly ... there's something up there, Karen. I can see it.'

The shaft was wide enough to stand up in if Slim squeezed himself in far enough. Karen was telling him to come out, that it was a job for the police, but Slim was adamant. He could see the light coming through the hole where the clock face had been, but something lodged further up the shaft was blocking most of it. Slim managed to get into a standing position. Stretching, he could just reach it—

'It's not Bob,' he said with a sigh, his shoulders sagging as he felt the object's lightness. It was large, made of canvas, and had something blocky inside. And then he realised.

'But I have found his bag.'

58

I⊤ ⊤ook them a while to manoeuvre the awkwardly shaped object down through the shaft and pull it out into the open air. It had got caught on a stone shelf protruding from the clock tower's inside wall, perhaps where part of the old ladder had been connected. It was certainly Bob's bag, containing several rigid pieces of wood that could fit together to form a pop-up puppet theatre. Slim found another bag too, one containing a sealed ziplock bag of opened letters, all written in a language Slim didn't understand.

Esperanto.

'Some of the envelopes are postmarked Argentina,' Karen said. 'This must be how they communicated. Their words hidden if anyone intercepted the letters. I mean, who would think it was Esperanto? Hardly a straightfor-ward choice for a hidden letter, is it?'

Slim said nothing. Standing beside the hole in the clock tower, the bag on the ground between them, it felt like someone was having a joke at their expense.

'Slim? What is it?'

'Here,' he said. 'This place was the best and the worst of him, but he had a connection to it that he could never fully break.' He remembered examining his photographs of Bob's house, one of which showed the kitchen mantelpiece, and an old photo of a boy on a pier walkway. Slim had glanced over it at the time, but had wondered afterwards if it was Bob, perhaps on a care home outing to the North Pier back before it closed. He had been smiling. He had told Karen about it, but the original had been lost in the house fire, meaning there was no way to know for sure.

'This pier ... it had a special meaning for him,' he said. 'He brought his secret things back here to hide them, back to the spot of the worst secret of all.'

'So why did he come back here the day that Reggie claimed to have seen him? And if Bob was here, how could Reggie have possibly seen him? Who did Reggie see?'

Slim walked back over to the collapsed pile of scaffolding, then turned and looked back towards the south. From here, the end of the great pier was visible, the old and the new separated by one almost continuous stretch of sand.

'We have to go back,' Slim said. 'I think I know just exactly what Reggie saw.'

∾

THEY WENT BY CAR. While Karen drove, Slim pulled out his notes and flicked through them, looking for the page he wanted. He folded the sheet into his pocket and put the rest away. When they parked near the promenade, Slim jumped out, Karen hurrying to keep up.

Richard Hardberry was standing outside his fish 'n' chips shop, a broom in his hand. A strong breeze raced across the beach, bringing with it a veil of sand. Richard scowled as he brushed it away.

'Mike,' he greeted Slim, who grimaced at Karen's puzzled look. 'Not done with your research yet, then?'

'Not quite,' Slim said. 'I have a question about Reggie Bowles … you said he wasn't actually employed down here, but he used to do odd jobs. What exactly did he used to do?'

Richard smiled. 'For the most part, we used to just lend him a spade and he'd get to work clearing the loose sand off the steps. It can cover them in a couple of hours on a dry, windy day.'

'That's what I wondered,' Slim said, heading for the steps without waiting to see if either Richard or Karen followed. He reached the exact spot where Reggie had claimed to have seen Bob's body. He knelt on the soft, billowing sand and began to shovel it away with both hands.

He was able to sink to his elbows before he got to colder, harder sand. Still, there was nothing. He moved a couple of feet to his right, knelt, began scooping again. Aware of Karen and Richard behind him, he began to dig harder.

Still nothing. He moved another couple of feet, began scooping again, his neck and face hot and prickly, both with exertion and the feeling of embarrassment that was slowly rising to the surface.

Karen put a hand on his shoulder. 'There's nothing—'

His fingers caught on something. Cloth. He dug around it, pulling back as it emerged out of the sand, feeling a sense of revulsion that wasn't quite enough to counter the momentary sense of triumph.

A human hand, badly decomposed, protruding from the end of an old coat.

'Oh my god,' Karen gasped. 'Is that—'

Slim stared at the human hand. 'Bob Harker,' he said. 'He was here all along.'

~

A CROWD HAD GATHERED at the edge of the police tape, although with several journalists as the police excavated Bob's remains inside a temporary tent. Slim and Karen stood nearby, sipping coffee Richard had kindly donated.

'You need to explain,' Karen said. 'I've been told by my boss that I have to make a statement to the press. What on earth do I say?'

'Tell them what you need to tell them,' Slim said. 'I'm sure there's more to the story.'

'How did you figure it out?'

He pulled a sheet of paper from his pocket. It was a medical report Donald Lane had sent him on Reggie Bowles. As well as delusional tendencies, Reggie had latter stage Alzheimer's. Slim had witnessed his forgetfulness in person.

'He went down there to dig out the steps,' Slim said. 'Then he found Bob's body. He covered Bob with sand to keep him safe, then went to get the police. By the time he returned he'd lost both his memory of Bob's exact location and that he'd covered him. He genuinely believed Bob had moved. If he had been precise with the location, the police might have noticed the disturbed sand, but as you saw, Bob was about fifteen feet from where Reggie remembered, and with Reggie being known to the police … you can see what happened.'

'But how did Bob get there?'

'He walked. I think you'll find when Bob's body is autopsied, there will be an accidental stab wound caused by one of the old scaffolding railings on the old pier. I believe Bob climbed up there, either to hide or retrieve something. The scaffolding collapsed, injuring him. Hurt and not thinking straight, he decided to walk back across the beach. It was misty but low tide. It was the only way he could have gone without being caught on any of the promenade CCTV cameras. Without his pack he would have just looked like any other old man. He was hurt, tired, and when he lay down near the steps, he passed away, probably from blood loss. And then Reggie found him.'

Karen was about to answer when a police officer emerged from the tent and called her over. When she returned a few minutes later she was shaking her head.

'There's definitely a touch of magic about you, Slim. They found something in Bob's clothes. A passport belonging to Maria-Luisa Gonzalez. There's also a hand-written note—in English, and signed by Maria-Luisa—explaining who she is and why she came to England.'

'He went to get it,' Slim said. 'He was walking home, making a direct beeline for his house. He wanted people to know who she was.'

Karen was quiet for a long time. At last, she said, 'It's beautiful in a way, isn't it? But at the same time, it's so very sad.'

Slim said nothing. He just stared out to sea, the wind ruffling his hair.

EPILOGUE

'You passed them all?'

Chris shrugged. 'Except art, but that's kind of a default since I didn't show up. Not sure I'll need that for anything anyway.' He grinned. 'It's all about expression, isn't that what they say?'

'Something like that. I've never dabbled in painting much myself.'

'Probably because your life is already a rich enough canvas,' Chris said.

'What?'

'My art teacher used to say that to all the rubbish kids.'

'I'm sure he never said that to you.'

'Only every other lesson. Not that it matters. I got my place.'

'College, is it?'

'I found one down in Exeter that offers A levels in history and sociology. Good for the police apparently. Although I might need to improve my physical skills a little. I'm thinking about taking up karate.'

'You'll be moving down there?'

'I've got an aunt that showed up out of the woodwork. She's offered me a room for a lot less than I'd have to pay on a flat. I think Granddad will be glad to see the back of me. I did go round there to tell him I was leaving but I don't think he realised I had even moved out. I hope he gets help. He might be a brute, but he's still my granddad.'

'I'll ask Karen to go round and offer him some advice,' Slim said. 'Anyway, it looks like your friends are waiting.' He nodded at a group of other kids standing nearby with their own results certificates in their hands. 'Exeter, eh. I often find myself down that way. We might run into each other. I promise not to put you in any danger.'

Chris leaned forward and pulled Slim into a hug. At first it was awkward, Chris's gangly frame difficult to hug back, but after a moment Slim leaned into it, and for a moment held the boy close, wondering if this was how it might have felt had he ever got to hug a son of his own. He let a tear bead in his eye, then quickly shook it off as they pulled away.

'You take care, Chris. Keep in touch.'

'And you, P.I. John "Slim" Hardy. I'll be watching the news for more of your stories.'

'I don't know about that,' Slim said, then briefly lifted a hand to wave as Chris headed off to his friends. Slim watched for a moment then turned away, looking out between the buildings to the sea. In the very far distance, the dark line of the North Pier was just visible, like a matchstick poking out into the water, set against a backdrop of grey.

Robert Tiller was still on remand, awaiting trial. More than a dozen associates had since been arrested and placed in custody. In an attempt to lessen his sentence, Jonathan Long had talked, naming names, blaming Tiller's coercion for Reggie's death, and even claiming that Reggie, during one of his turns, had claimed to have buried someone near the Grand Pier. He had thought it nonsense until Slim discovered Bob Harker's remains.

And for Bob Harker, Slim's theory had proven correct, as far as Karen could work out. He had hidden personal items belonging to Maria-Luisa out on the pier, and had apparently gone out there to retrieve them, perhaps before revealing her body. He had climbed up on some old scaffolding railings, only to have them collapse. Traces of tissue and clothing on a rusted section of broken railing, as well as a coinciding injury to Bob's torso, confirmed this, although his official cause of death was recorded as heart failure due to blood loss.

Slim walked from Chris's school down to the beach. The summer had come late, but the forecast offered a couple of weeks of decent weather for the kids and their families down on the sand. As he stood by the top of the steps down on to the promenade, he almost considered going down, but changed his mind. He had never really been much of a beach person.

James Jackson had got off with a warning and community service. According to Karen, he had enrolled in college for September. Samuel Owens had got a suspended sentence for theft and obstructing a police investigation. His girlfriend, a naïve but overall innocent party, had got off with a sound dressing-down from both Karen and then more terrifyingly Amanda Smart, for not being honest about her sources. After much deliberation, including with the police, it had been decided to move forward with the play, but credit Bob Harker as its writer.

Standing at the top of the beach, with the Grand Pier in front of him, and the old North Pier visible in the distance, Slim gave a slow nod. He was done here. He had other cases to consider: perhaps a simple fraud or a marital dispute might make a nice change after nearly getting himself and someone else killed. He would get a coffee somewhere and think things over.

With a sigh, he turned away from the sea and took his phone out from his pocket. He glanced down at the two missed calls from earlier in the day, both from Karen. He had told her he was visiting for a couple of days to see Chris pick up his results, but they had made no other plans. His finger lingered over the redial button, wondering whether he should call her back.

THE END

ABOUT THE AUTHOR

Jack Benton is a pen name of Chris Ward, the author of the dystopian *Tube Riders* series, the horror/science fiction *Tales of Crow* series, and the *Endinfinium* YA fantasy series. He also writes seasonal romance as CP Ward, as well as a few other things.

Along the Old Pier is the tenth mystery to feature John "Slim" Hardy. There will be more…

Chris would love to hear from you:
www.amillionmilesfromanywhere.net/tokyolost
chrisward@amillionmilesfromanywhere.net

ACKNOWLEDGMENTS

Many thanks to Becky and Elizabeth. And as always, to my muses, Jenny Twist and John Dalton.

Finally, for those of you who support me via Patreon, thanks very much. In no special order: Donna Askins, Mike Wright, Rosemary Kenny, Jane Ornelas, Ron, Gail Beth Le Vine, Jennie Brown, Janet Hodgson, Karen P, Paul Go, Sharon Kenneson, and Dr. Kat Crispin.

And for everyone who's **Bought me a Coffee** recently: Janie Fillman, Sheila Rutledge, Wandawoof, Andi Kreth, irholl35, Lynn, Lisa Randall, Kay Frederickart, Bruce Schhlliger, Theresa, and Norma. Thank you. Your support means so much.

Last and not least, to all my readers. Thank you for supporting my books and I look forward to bringing you the next John "Slim" Hardy adventure.

JB

November 2025

Printed in Dunstable, United Kingdom